Abaddon

ELIZABETH DONALD

Cerridwen Press

What the critics are saying...

ଔ

WINNER OF THE 2008 DARRELL AWARD!

"This story is not a romance by any means. But it is a story of loss and revenge. A story of love and a hate that has lasted for a hundred years and that will not be denied. It is a story of fire. The fire of the human and the vampire hearts. A story of a hate that must be stopped or the vampire and human friendships that are barely holding on will be shattered because vampire consorts are being killed and someone wants the vampires to take the blame […] a storytelling ability to rival that of Stephen King." ~ *Enchanting Reviews*

"*Abaddon* is a remarkable book and the *Nocturnal Urges* series are some of the best fiction novels I've read in a while. Elizabeth Donald is an author of superior caliber who crafted a multi-faceted story with socially relevant themes and characters that I will remember for a long time to come. These people were very real to me and I felt genuine emotion for them and for what they were experiencing. Ms. Donald is now an auto buy author for me and I am quite looking forward to more from her *Nocturnal Urges* series." ~ *Fallen Angel Reviews*

"This story is gripping and raw with intense emotion and great characters. […] This vampire world and its characters are created so realistically you almost expect to hear about them on the evening news, and not be able to sleep afterwards."
~ *Coffee Time Romance Reviews*

A Cerridwen Press Publication

www.cerridwenpress.com

Abaddon

ISBN 9781419957970
ALL RIGHTS RESERVED.
Abaddon Copyright © 2007 Elizabeth Donald.
Edited by Mary Moran.
Cover art by Syneca.

This book printed in the U.S.A. by Jasmine-Jade Enterprises, LLC.

Electronic book Publication September 2007
Trade paperback Publication August 2008

With the exception of quotes used in reviews, this book may not be reproduced or used in whole or in part by any means existing without written permission from the publisher, Ellora's Cave Publishing Inc., 1056 Home Avenue, Akron, OH 44310-3502.

Warning: The unauthorized reproduction or distribution of this copyrighted work is illegal. Criminal copyright infringement, including infringement without monetary gain, is investigated by the FBI and is punishable by up to 5 years in federal prison and a fine of $250,000.
(http://www.fbi.gov/ipr/)

This book is a work of fiction and any resemblance to persons, living or dead, or places, events or locales is purely coincidental. The characters are productions of the author's imagination and used fictitiously.

Cerridwen Press is an imprint of Ellora's Cave Publishing, Inc.®

ABADDON

Trademarks Acknowledgement

☙

The author acknowledges the trademarked status and trademark owners of the following wordmarks mentioned in this work of fiction:

Batman: DC Comics Warner Communications Inc.

Boy Scouts: The National Boy Scouts of America Foundation

Ford: Ford Motor Company

Ritz: The Ritz Hotel, Limited Corporation

Acknowledgement

To Firefighter Brian Pfeiffer of the Mercerville, N J., Fire Department for his advice on the nature of firefighting, rescue and arson investigation. Talking to Brian was much preferable to looking up books titled How to Kill People With Fire and Get Away With It and was much less likely to result in a search warrant for my apartment. Seriously, if I got it right, it was thanks to Brian. If I got it wrong, it's because I wasn't listening when he told me. In the years I have spent covering fires and talking with firefighters, I have found that they rarely consider themselves heroes for the work that they do—it's a job, nothing more. They are wrong.

To the Memphis Police Department for answering my silly questions. To my family for being eternal cheerleaders. To David Wallsh and Tony Price for helping me build better human traps. To Devin Harris for her beautiful designs. To Chris Smith for picking Danny's Christmas present. To Angelia Sparrow for the right line at the right time. To the Rivendell Gang for being groupies. To Becky Zoole for the Hebrew translation and meanings of the word Abaddon.

Special thanks to the Sleepwalkers—Kit Tunstall, Jeff Strand, Jay Smith and Frank Fradella, and to Anne Freitas, Kelly Parker, Dana Franks, Ray Barrington, Joann Betschart, Jon Flanigan, Michael Hickerson, Drew and Sarah Sanford, Vernard Martin, Patrick Stubblefield and Melodee Britt. More than any other to date, this was a collaborative effort. You all supported me through the construction of this book and allowed me to mangle your names and kill you in gruesome ways. It's how I show my love.

Kudos to my editor Mary Moran, for making the magic happen once more. Mary has that special gift of finding my mistakes and making me laugh at them—but still making me fix them. I am always grateful for her partnership.

Most especially, thanks to my wonderful son Ian. for putting up with that darn laptop all the time.

Prologue

1873

෩

Cold rain fell on the cobblestones, mixing with the blood in the alley behind Saint Bartholomew's Church.

Sister Mary put the kettle on the stove, hoping that in a moment the screech of the steam would block out the screams in the alleys and tenements behind the church. She dared a peek out between the window shutters and immediately wished she hadn't. The smoke rose anew from burning hovels in the vampire quarters that filled the narrow streets behind Saint Bartholomew's, rising into the dark sky.

Out of the smoke she saw a man dragging step after step through the uneven cobblestone alley toward the church. He was carrying the body of a woman, drenched in rain and blood.

Quickly Sister Mary ran to the rear door, throwing it open to a rush of rain and wind. As he came closer, she recognized Martin, the quiet black man who helped Mr. Crockett with the grounds around Saint Bartholomew's. In his arms...it could not be Melody, Martin's sweet wife? The skin of her bared shoulder, normally the color of coffee with the slightest touch of cream, was blackened and blistered, streams of garish-red blood leaking through the crinkled burns.

"Sister, please," Martin pleaded. "Let us in."

Theresa, a young novitiate, appeared in the hallway with Sister Mary. "Come in, Martin," Sister Mary said, and moved to take Melody from him. The poor man was covered in blood and seemed about to fall down.

The novitiate stood still in the doorway. Sister Mary shot a glance over at her. "Theresa, you come over here and help now."

Theresa sidled past Martin and helped lift Melody's legs. As they carried Melody through the doorway, Theresa whispered, "I thought they couldn't enter a church."

"Be silent, girl," Sister Mary said in a tone more harsh than she intended.

Martin made the sign of the cross before he entered the abbey.

Sister Mary lay Melody out on the kitchen table as another scream rose from the vampire quarters. "There is evil in this city tonight," she said, checking the kettle. "Are you well?"

"I'll be all right, ma'am," Martin said, dropping into a kitchen chair. "I stopped them before they finished Melody."

Theresa gasped. "You struck them? Humans?"

Martin dropped his eyes. "White humans, ma'am."

"Theresa, go and wake the father," Sister Mary commanded, and the girl gratefully fled from the kitchen. "You must forgive the girl, Martin. She is new to the city and has just begun preparation for vows. I believe you and Melody are the first vampires she has ever seen. All this is strange to her."

"Strange to me too, ma'am," Martin said. "We don't carry the yellow fever. They must know that."

The kettle began to screech and Sister Mary quickly poured it into a small bowl. She began to clean the rain and dirt from Melody's wounds with the heated wet cloth. "They know nothing," she said forcefully. "They know they are afraid, they are dying, and you are…"

"Safe," Martin said, and made a tired, sarcastic sound that was almost a laugh. "From the fever, at least." It hurt Sister Mary's heart a little to hear such defeat in Martin's voice. He was always cheerful, a quiet man who ignored the terrible things people would say to him as he went about his job on the church grounds.

Suddenly there was another pounding at the back door. Martin was on his feet instantly as Sister Mary swept past him to the door.

"We know there's one in there, Sister!" a hoarse voice rose. It was Crockett, well-drunk by the sound of it, and there were others with him. Torchbearers. Sister Mary could smell the sweet, hideous scent of burning flesh and wood wafting from the quarters through the church windows.

"Be on your way, Mr. Crockett! This is the house of the Lord!" Sister Mary commanded through the door.

Behind her, she saw Martin pick up Melody's unmoving form and disappear into the church.

Father Sweeney raced down the hallway, uncharacteristically clad in a dressing gown. Sister Mary could not recall ever seeing the austere priest in anything other than his black robes.

"This is God's sanctuary!" the priest shouted through the door. "You shall not bring evil here!"

They slammed something against the wooden door. It began to splinter right away. Father Sweeney pulled Sister Mary back just in time as the door broke free. Behind them, the nuns had come, standing together in the small foyer. Crockett stood there with at least nine large men, smelling of burnt wood and whiskey.

"This is a sanctuary!" Father Sweeney protested again, and they shoved him out of the way. Theresa stumbled backward and burst into tears, but the other nuns stood together in trembling resolve. The men ignored them, shoving them inside. They overturned tables and wrenched open large cabinets, storming into the warm, quiet abbey with their boots and cloaks soaked in rain and blood.

Sister Mary ran after Crockett toward the church sanctuary, praying that Martin had found a place to hide in the attic. But when she passed through the stone archway, her heart sank.

Between the gleaming white pillars, Martin knelt alone before the marble altar, murmuring prayer. The statues of saints looked down on him, their faces shrouded in shadow. Above him, the golden cross gleamed mellow and serene in the flickering candlelight.

Father Sweeney stumbled in from the hallway next to Sister Mary, a thin trickle of blood staining his forehead. Crockett surged forward.

"No!" Sister Mary protested, pulling at Crockett's arm, but he pulled away easily and used his torch to club Martin over the head before the altar.

"This thing don't deserve sanctuary!" Crockett shouted to Sister Mary as several more of his friends shoved past her into the church. "It's him and his kind brought the sickness! They'll rule this earth when we're all dead if'n we don't stop it!"

Crockett dragged Martin's unresisting form down the aisle. Father Sweeney ran after him, grabbing for Martin's arm in a hideous tug-of-war beneath the saddened eyes of the saints, watching in dark reflections from the stained-glass windows.

Then one of the torchbearers struck Father Sweeney— *struck the priest right in the house of the Lord,* Sister Mary's mind whispered to her in horror—and they dragged Martin out of the church.

Sister Mary ran out the church door to the white marble steps outside, now stained with Martin's blood. They were beating him with sticks and rocks, kicking him with their large boots on the lawn in front of the church. "Stop! Stop, you're killing him!" she cried. "Help! Someone, please help!"

There was no one. The streets were empty save for a single shadow of a man vanishing back into the warren of slums beyond the reach of the streetlights. No one would be caught out of doors on this night of insanity, and no one would come to help a stranger. A black man. A vampire.

"There is blood on the church!" Sister Mary screamed, and for a second, she had their attention. She stood before the dark sanctuary above the streaks of Martin's blood, garishly bright against the white marble. Tears streamed from her eyes. "If you do this, his blood is on you! On all of us! Forever!"

That seemed to catch them for just a second. Then Martin's eyes opened. Crockett let out a scream borne of fury and fear and shoved a torch into Martin's midsection.

"No!" Sister Mary screamed, but they ignored her, jabbing at the flailing vampire with their own torches, shouting and cheering as his skin began to burn. Martin screamed, and the sound of his scream echoed down the cobblestone street and through Sister Mary into the church itself, seeming to echo inside her heart as it grew inside the church behind her.

The fire lit up the front of Saint Bartholomew's in dancing shadows and darkness, casting an unearthly jittering glow into the sanctuary. Unable to watch any longer, Sister Mary turned away from the horrible vision on the steps.

Behind the altar, the woman Sister Mary had known as Melody rose up, her blackened skin bleeding anew beneath the tattered remains of her dress. She stepped before the cross itself, moving down the aisle in the dancing glow cast by her husband's fire.

She walked past the staggering Father Sweeney, stopping beside Sister Mary's pleading, tearful face. She watched the fire and the unheeding men cheering it, and it lit in her own dark, unfathomable eyes.

Chapter One

ઝ

Ryan dipped Isabel before the crackling fireplace as the pounding guitars and drums filled their living room, her dark hair nearly sweeping the hardwood floor.

"No more will my green sea go turn a deeper blue… I could not foresee this thing happening to you…" sang the Rolling Stones as they danced across the floor.

Danny and Samantha spun around as Parker and Chapman tried hopelessly to keep up. The couches had been pushed back to make room for dancing between the glittering Christmas tree and the stone fireplace.

"No fair!" Chapman called as Ryan lifted Isabel back to her feet. "You probably studied with Arthur Murray or something!"

Ryan suddenly switched to a waltz, sweeping Isabel across the room in perfect four-step strangely timed to the Rolling Stones. Isabel burst out laughing. "He's just showing off!" she declared.

Samantha started to jitterbug in the middle of the floor, her dress swinging about her legs. Danny tried to copy her movements for about six beats then he just jumped straight up and down as she giggled. "No fair!" he echoed.

Ryan spied Celia standing against the wall, arms folded as the rest of them danced in the firelight. He winked at Isabel and let her spin away, reaching out to Celia. The teenager gave him a strange, unreadable look then took his hand. He started an easy dance around the floor.

"This music came out forever ago, you know that," Celia said.

"Tin Pan Alley was forever ago, kid," Ryan said, grinning. "This song came out yesterday."

Isabel flopped onto the couch next to Anne Freitas in a flounce of burgundy velvet, its rich darkness complementing her dark hair and eyes. "Whew," she said, fanning herself. "I can't keep up with him. He doesn't have to breathe."

"That could come in handy," Freitas cracked, waggling her eyebrows. "Lots of stamina."

Isabel smacked her friend lightly on the arm. "I should warn Danny what he's getting himself into," she said, watching Danny and Samantha dance. "At least he's only stuck with the dances from the twentieth century. You should hear Ryan get all maudlin over the Irish folk-songs collection I gave him. It's pathetic really."

"I heard that!" Ryan called out.

Danny moved over to Celia, spinning her away from Ryan. "My turn!" he grinned. Ryan pretended to throw a punch and Danny ducked, laughing. Celia let out an uncharacteristic giggle as Danny danced her away and Samantha joined Ryan.

"Celia's boyfriend wouldn't come?" Isabel murmured to Freitas.

"Parker told her to bring him," Freitas replied, rolling her eyes. "Celia's exact words were, 'Lucas don't do that sort of shit'. I smell trouble around that boy."

"Oh Annie, you don't like anybody to be happy," Isabel teased. "And where is Frank tonight?"

Freitas shot her a look.

Ryan and Samantha began some complicated dance that left the humans in the dust. The Rolling Stones went into their final driving drumbeats with Freitas and Isabel clapping in time. Samantha whirled in her powder-blue silk dress, her corn-silk blonde hair a direct contrast to Ryan's dark Irish curls. They moved around each other in perfect timing, their dance some long-lost folk rhythm that perfectly matched the rock music coming from the stereo.

Ryan picked up Samantha and spun her around in a circle as the music faded and the others burst into applause.

"No more, I'm wasted!" Parker said breathlessly, leaning on Chapman. For once her dark red hair was tousled around her shoulders instead of bound up in a tight braid.

"Aw, c'mon," Samantha teased.

"In the old days, we wouldn't stop until the sun came up," Ryan said, grinning.

"In the old days, you didn't have indoor plumbing or electric lights," Isabel teased.

"Presents!" Parker insisted. Danny chortled a little and Samantha nudged him hard, meeting Parker's look with an innocent smile.

They settled on the overstuffed couches facing each other on either side of the large fireplace. On the wall over the fireplace rested a lovely painting of an Irish waterfall, Freitas and Parker's housewarming gift when Ryan and Isabel moved into this small house on the outskirts of Memphis. They had tried living in Isabel's midtown apartment for a while, but after painting over the word LEECH on their front door four times and replacing Isabel's slashed tires twice, they decided they weren't cut out for city life.

Isabel pulled a fuzzy Santa hat down over her hair, sitting on the floor in front of the Christmas tree's sparkling white lights. "Get the list, Annie!" she commanded.

Freitas stood, digging a piece of paper out of her purse. "Next time, you organize the Secret Santas," she chided Isabel. "I'm a busy woman."

"Yeah, putting the bad guys away. Most of the time," Samantha teased.

"Watch it, missy, I've got handcuffs," Freitas returned.

Abaddon

Parker murmured something to Chapman, who burst out laughing beside her on the couch. Freitas shot them both a look and they practiced sitting up straight with Cheshire-cat grins.

Freitas rolled her eyes. "Children," she muttered. "Samantha first."

Samantha joined Isabel on the floor in front of the Christmas tree, digging out a square package. "I drew Michael," she said, handing the present to Chapman. "I had to enlist some help."

"Cops are easy to buy for," Freitas said. "We want peace and goodwill toward men."

"Yeah, that's real easy," Celia said sarcastically from her perch on the couch arm. She never seemed comfortable sitting in chairs, always standing or leaning somewhere as though she were about to run or fight. Celia was in a black silk dress that matched Parker's, but while Parker seemed nearly as comfortable as she was in jeans, Celia moved awkwardly, not sure of herself.

Chapman pulled the last of the wrapping paper off and a big smile spread across his cheerful face. "Damn. Thanks, Samantha."

"Thank Kelly," Samantha said, pointing at Parker. "I have no idea what I bought."

Chapman held up the box. "It's a top-notch backpacking stove, a hell of a lot better and lighter than that clunky thing I've been dragging around since Boy Scouts."

Parker laughed, leaning on his arm. "I knew you were a Boy Scout, I just knew it."

Freitas sat back down. "So, Chapman, now it's your turn."

"You can call me Michael, *Detective*," Chapman said, moving over to the tree.

"I'm her partner and she still calls me by my last name," Parker groused.

Chapman pulled out a smaller box. "And I had no help whatsoever in this," he said, handing the box to Freitas. "I had to guess."

Freitas pulled at the ribbon. Then she grinned.

"Well, that's better than I expected," Chapman said, scooting back over to sit on the floor in front of Parker.

Freitas held up a complete kit of gun-cleaning supplies designed for her service pistol.

Parker laughed out loud. "Perfect," she said, massaging Chapman's shoulders.

"I guess that makes it my turn," Freitas said, leaning forward to pull a small square box from under the tree's soft glowing lights. "Catch!"

She tossed the box to Danny, who caught it easily. He opened it and let out a squawk.

"What?" Samantha asked, peering over his shoulder.

"Ozzie Smith!" Danny exclaimed, holding an autographed baseball encased in a plastic cube over his head. "Damn! Thanks, Anne!"

"No problem," Freitas said easily.

Danny examined the signature closely, grinning. "You've got to understand, if you were a fan in the eighties…"

"You were an Ozzie Smith fan," Samantha finished. "I remember."

Danny kept turning the baseball over in his hand until Samantha elbowed him. "It's your turn, sweet."

"Sorry," Danny said, scrambling over to the tree. "I really got stuck, so apologies for this in advance."

He handed a rectangular box to Parker. She pulled off the golden bow and opened it. Then she threw the bow at Danny, who batted it away with a laugh.

"What? What is it?" Freitas asked.

Parker stood and held the white T-shirt against her chest. It read, "I Got Bitten at Nocturnal Urges and All I Got Was This Lousy T-Shirt".

Chapman started to choke. After two beats, everyone burst out laughing. Danny cowered in mock fear before the Christmas tree as Parker mimed a punch at him.

"It's our biggest seller," Ryan said, grinning.

"I can never wear this in public, you know that," Parker said. "I've never even been inside the club!"

Danny shrugged. "Hey, maybe you and Michael would like to go on an excursion sometime," he said, waggling his eyebrows.

"I highly recommend it," Isabel grinned, patting Ryan's knee.

Parker blushed hard as she sat back down.

"It's your turn," Chapman said to her with a grin.

"Shut up," Parker returned, getting back up and pulling a package from the tree. She handed it to Samantha. "Use it to club your man a few times, wouldja?"

Samantha was still giggling as she pulled off the paper. "Oh Lord," she said. "Would you believe I don't even have a copy of this?"

Danny looked up the book in her hand. "*Dracula*," he said, snickering. "Oh man. You got your own back, Kelly."

"Hey, this isn't a first edition, is it?" Samantha asked, examining the title page of the worn black book.

Parker snorted. "You overestimate an honest cop's salary," she said. "But it's an early edition. I know how you like older books."

"Thank you," Samantha said, smiling. "Even if Stoker was an ass."

"Hey, Samantha already went," Isabel said. "Who goes next?"

"You, since you're so eager," Danny said, grinning.

Isabel reached under the tree and withdrew a gaily wrapped package. "For Celia," she said, holding it out to the lanky teen.

Celia looked up, startled. She glanced over at Parker, who smiled encouragingly. Celia took the package hesitantly and pulled at the heavy velvet bow. The wrapping paper fell to the floor and Celia looked up at Isabel.

"It's a journal," Isabel said. "Something for you to write down your thoughts and feelings where no one can see them."

Celia opened the tapestry-bound volume and thumbed open the cream-white pages. "That's real nice," she said quietly. "Thanks."

"You're welcome, sweetheart," Isabel said.

"That means it's your turn," Parker said to Celia.

Celia met Parker's eyes, rubbing her hand nervously through her spiky black hair. "Mine's dumb," she said.

Parker didn't say anything, but her eyes communicated wordlessly with Celia. The girl scooted forward and pulled a small round tin from under the tree. It had a lopsided red bow stuck to the top.

"I didn't know what to get," she said, casting her eyes down. She nearly shoved the tin at Ryan then skittered back over to her perch on the arm of the couch.

Ryan opened the tin and the smell of chocolate floated out. Inside were at least two dozen chocolate cookies with dark chocolate chips.

"Oh Celia, you hit the mark," Isabel said, smiling. "Never saw a man love chocolate so much."

"Thank you, Celia," Ryan said. "Did you make these yourself?"

"Sure did," Parker said. "Made a complete mess of our kitchen too."

"And cleaned it up," Celia retorted.

"Cleaner than it was before," Chapman said, and Parker stopped massaging his shoulders long enough to smack him on top of his head. "Ow!"

"Okay, that leaves Callahan," Freitas said, grinning mischievously.

"Hey, Ryan did not draw Isabel!" Samantha protested. "No way!"

Danny grinned, scooting out of Ryan's way. "I suspect the draw was fixed."

"I demand an investigation!" Parker called.

"Would you people shut up?" Freitas said. "Callahan has a present to give. Stand up, Isabel."

Isabel stood, a faint smile on her face. Ryan knelt down and pulled a tiny box from the branches inside the tree. "I didn't want you to see it until now," he said, brushing a few pine needles off the box before he opened it.

Then Ryan knelt before Isabel and held up a silver claddagh ring set with a small blue stone for the heart.

"Oh my," Samantha whispered. Danny held her hand, smiling.

"Isabel," Ryan said. "I can think of no better company in which to ask you to spend your life with me, to be my consort and to live our lives together as one, 'til death do us part."

Isabel slowly drew the Santa hat off her head, tears brimming in her eyes. She reached out to Ryan, touching the side of his face tenderly.

"Answer!" Parker called.

"Yes, of course yes," Isabel said, smiling through tears.

Ryan stood and tried to slide the ring onto her finger. His hands were trembling and she had to help him a bit.

"Crown out, that means you're taken," Freitas said.

"You're shaking," Isabel said, taking Ryan's hands in hers. "What did you think I was going to say?"

"Let's just say I'm relieved," Ryan murmured.

"Oh for God's sake, kiss her!" Danny yelled.

Ryan obliged and the kiss went on for some time. Isabel's arms wrapped around Ryan's neck as he held her close. The others applauded, and when they stopped, Ryan and Isabel were still kissing.

"All right, all right, get a room," Parker teased.

"We're in their room—well, their house," Chapman said.

Freitas shushed them and they could all hear Isabel whisper, "I love you," in Ryan's ear. When they finally let go and sat back down on the hearth, still holding hands, there was more applause. Isabel kept looking at the ring, sliding a finger over the stone as if in wonder.

"Now I know the draw was fixed," Danny accused Freitas, wagging a finger.

"Reluctantly," Ryan said, grinning at Freitas. "You'd think she was Isabel's mother."

"No, my mother would have liked you," Isabel said, smiling.

"I like Callahan just fine," Freitas said defensively.

Isabel grinned. "As well as you like anybody you've arrested."

Samantha raised her hand, smiling.

Freitas rolled her eyes. "I didn't arrest you either, missy."

"Well, it was close," Parker murmured. "Who knows, maybe someday you'll even be able to marry."

"Don't get me started," Danny groused.

Samantha stood, reaching for the glass of wine she had been drinking. "A toast!" she said, and everyone reached for their glasses, mostly empty. She moved over to the sideboard, pouring a few refills. Danny came over to help, and when her hand shook, he caught a glass before it could tip. He looked at her and her eyes seemed troubled.

"You okay?" he asked.

Samantha nodded and her eyes cleared as they passed the glasses out. They rose up before the fire, glasses held together. Parker glanced around for Celia but the girl was nowhere to be seen.

"To good friends, to the holiday," Samantha said, nodding toward the three police officers. "And especially to my dear friend Ryan, who has found his match in Isabel, in more ways than one! May they have a long and happy life together."

"Hear, hear," Danny said, and they clinked glasses.

When the drinks were gone and the wrapping paper shoved into a trash can, Samantha and Danny put on their coats. "Merry Christmas," Samantha said, hugging Isabel.

Danny shook Ryan's hand. "Congratulations," he said, smiling.

"Drive safe," Ryan said as they stepped out into the night. Snow was falling, quiet and lovely in the cold December night. Danny helped Samantha step carefully over the slick walk to their car.

"That's our cue," Freitas said. Parker and Chapman already had their coats on, exchanging farewells.

"Where's Celia?" Isabel asked, looking back into the kitchen. The back door was slightly ajar. "Did she leave?"

Parker sighed. "She does the disappearing thing a lot," she said. "She's coming along really. She'll turn up late tonight in her room and I'll have no idea how she got in or out."

"She just needs a little time," Isabel said. "I'm glad she's staying with you."

"Sort of," Parker said. "When I can find her. I live in fear that Children's Services is going to show up sometime when she's pulled a disappearing act. I want to keep her out of the system if at all possible."

Freitas stepped to the doorway, adjusting her coat. She pulled Isabel into an uncharacteristic hug. "Congratulations, Isabel," she said, her voice affected. "I wish you all the happiness in the world."

Isabel returned the hug, and when she let go, her eyes were shining.

"What was in that eggnog?" Chapman wondered.

Freitas chucked him hard in the arm. "Shaddup," she said. "Parker's driving."

"Damn skippy," Parker replied.

The three made their way down the walkway into the snow. Freitas glanced back and saw Isabel leaning against Ryan's chest, his arm around her as they both waved goodbye before closing the door.

They reached Parker's battered Ford and Freitas climbed into the backseat while Parker turned the key in the ignition.

Nothing happened.

"You're kidding," Chapman said, sliding into the passenger seat.

"Too cold," Parker said, trying again. "Maybe the battery?"

Freitas huddled in her thick winter coat. "I knew we should have taken my car," she said.

"Oh shush," Parker said, peering at the dashboard as though she could will it into behaving. Chapman got out of the car and went around to the front. Parker popped the hood and he lifted it into place.

"What's he going to do, jump-start it with his magic heat vision?" Freitas said.

"He'll stare at it for five minutes and then we'll call the auto club," Parker said.

Freitas looked up at the house, where most of the lights were out. "I bet Ryan could give us a jump."

Parker snickered. "I think Ryan plans to jump something else tonight."

Freitas rolled her eyes. But whatever she planned to say was interrupted by the screeching siren that blatted from under Parker's hood.

Freitas and Parker jumped out of the car to stand next to Chapman, who was fiddling around with a few wires. He looked up at Parker's annoyed face. "Oops."

"Oops," Parker repeated, scanning the empty street. Fortunately there were few neighbors this far out.

"I may have to arrest you for causing a disturbance," Freitas said, peering at the engine.

"I'm pretty sure it's..." Chapman's voice trailed off as he wrenched a connection into place. The car alarm stopped.

"Thank God," Parker said. "Don't suppose it'll start now?"

Chapman turned back to Parker with a grin, but whatever smart-ass reply he was about to give died on his lips. He stared over Parker's head toward the house.

Parker and Freitas followed his gaze to the house where dark smoke was drifting from under the front door. The windows were entirely black. Faintly, they could hear smoke alarms blaring inside the house.

"Shit!" Parker shouted, already reaching into the car for her police band radio. "Dead!"

Freitas ran toward the burning house. Parker ran after her as Chapman fumbled out his cell phone.

"Annie, wait!" Parker shouted.

Freitas reached the front door and tried to open it but it was locked. She pounded hard on the door. "Isabel! Isabel, open up!"

The heat grew intense as Parker reached the porch, some of the snow melting in a rush of filthy water past her feet. Freitas grabbed a paving stone out of the garden and hauled it back to break the window beside the door.

Parker grabbed her arm.

"Let me go, goddammit!" Freitas shouted.

"You can't do that!" Parker yelled back. "It'll make it worse!"

Chapman scrambled up toward them. "ETA three minutes," he yelled, waving the cell phone.

Freitas shoved Parker away and ran around the side of the house, stumbling in the foot-deep snow. Parker followed her but when Chapman tried to go after them, she motioned him back. "Wait for them," she said.

Freitas struggled through the snow past blackened windows leaking tendrils of smoke around their frames, dense smoke billowing out between the siding into the sky. The smell of burning wood was intense and Parker coughed as she tromped around the house after Freitas.

Around the back, Freitas was running faster, her feet sinking into the loose snow. A body lay on the ground between the house and the garage, blood staining the snow.

It was Ryan, unconscious, blood leaking from a gash on the side of his head. The back door was open, but the kitchen beyond was a mass of dense black smoke.

Freitas stepped over Ryan and tried to push her way into the kitchen, roiling smoke in her face. Parker pulled her back again, dragging her away from the doorway where flames began to lick the wood.

"Goddammit, let me go!" Freitas shouted.

"Stop it! You can't go in there!" Parker shouted. "EMS will be here any second and it'll only be that much harder if they have to save you as well as Isabel!"

Freitas swung a fist at her and Parker blocked it, grabbing her arm. "Dammit!" Freitas yelled, pushing her partner, but Parker wouldn't let go. Freitas fought her until she was leaning on Parker's arm, her fists clenched inside her gloves.

"You can't, Annie," Parker said, more quietly.

Freitas let go of Parker without looking at her and knelt beside Ryan. Parker coughed in the smoke boiling out the open door. "Is he alive?"

"What, you suggest I take his pulse?" Freitas snapped. "He's a vampire."

Parker stood and pulled out her cell phone. But instead of making a call, she switched on the camera function and began taking pictures.

"What the hell are you doing?" Freitas asked.

"Preserving evidence," Parker said, pointing at the snow. Beyond Ryan's unconscious form, tracks led away from the door toward the woods behind the house. "EMS will track that all over."

"Track..." Freitas froze for a moment. "Shit, Parker!" She ran along the tracks, stumbling a little as the icy snow water leaked into her heels. She reached the edge of the woods behind Ryan and Isabel's house, fumbling in her purse for her service pistol.

The woods were silent and dark. Nothing seemed to breathe within it. The tracks stopped at the edge of the woods.

A faint siren echoed in the distance.

"Annie, dammit, get back up here!" Parker said, checking Ryan again. His eyelids moved a little—he was still alive.

"No one," Freitas murmured, her weapon still leveled at the shadows.

The sirens grew louder and finally the flashing red lights reflected on the snow around the house, now lit with its own sickly orange glow. Parker ran as fast as she could to the front yard, waving at the paramedics, and they ran past her with a gurney carried between them above the snow. Two firefighters in full apparatus followed them, disappearing into the black cloud that filled the kitchen.

Chapman was talking quickly to the scene commander, a burly man with the name of the local volunteer house stenciled on his helmet. Two firefighters were already breaking in the front door as the hose teams poured water on the sides and roof.

"What happened?" the scene commander asked.

"Unknown cause, had to have started in the last ten minutes," Parker said, tromping toward them with her shield held up. "One's outside, head trauma, your guys are on it. The other's presumably still in the house. Woman, late twenties."

"Shit," the scene commander said. "I got two teams in there, Detective. We'll find her."

Freitas followed back around the house with the paramedics, who carried Ryan on a gurney.

"He's a vamp, we gotta take him to Saint Abraham's in the city," one of the paramedics told the scene commander.

"That's at least half an hour from here!" Parker yelled. "There's another person in the house who's gonna need you!"

"Vamp?" the scene commander asked.

Parker resisted the urge to clout him. "Human," she spat. "Ryan's stable, order your men to wait."

The paramedics started to move past them toward the ambulance and Freitas stepped in front of them. "Try to leave and I will fucking—"

"Annie!" Parker warned, and Freitas shut up.

No one spoke for a few minutes as the streams of water turned the black, billowing smoke into clouds of steam. The paramedics loaded Ryan onto their ambulance but waited outside with the scene commander.

Two firefighters appeared in the front doorway, dragging something behind them. When they reached the porch they lifted it up and Parker saw the dim outline of a woman's body.

"Oh Jesus," breathed the scene commander as he motioned the paramedics over.

For a moment Parker thought there was nothing wrong with Isabel as they lay her out on the gurney. There were faint traces of soot around her nose and mouth, and her hair seemed slightly singed. The smell of smoke drifted from her. But her face and skin were unmarked. It was as though she were only sleeping.

Then they moved the oxygen tank and Parker saw a deep, bloody gash in the side of her neck. Her burgundy dress was stained a deeper red with a spreading dark stain of blood.

A paramedic pressed an oxygen mask to her face while the other checked her breathing. No one spoke as they began compressing her chest. The one holding the mask talked into his radio and an on-call emergency doctor began giving him instructions from some unseen, safe place with linoleum and overhead lights.

Parker winced when they ripped open the bodice of Isabel's velvet dress, tearing off her white lace bra to place electroshock pads against her chest. The snow fell on her bare skin. She seemed so defenseless, violated in her own home, on her own front lawn. There was something sad and pathetic about her bare body lying exposed in the cold air in front of all these strangers.

The paramedic shocked her and Isabel's whole body jumped. He shocked her again and her arm slid off the gurney, hanging in midair. Parker made a small noise in her throat and Chapman tried to hold her hand. Parker glanced over at Freitas, who stood immobile as a stone carving, watching the paramedics work as the flame light danced in her eyes.

Then the paramedic looked up at the scene commander and shook his head.

"Sonofabitch," the scene commander murmured. "I'm sorry, Detective."

Freitas paid him no attention. She didn't try to stop the paramedics as they climbed into the ambulance with Ryan.

Parker came up beside Freitas and tried to touch her shoulder. She jerked away with a pained, hurt sound deep in her throat that Parker could feel in her heart.

Then Freitas turned to the scene commander, steel and ice again. "Do you have an arson investigator on your staff?" she asked.

"No, ma'am," he replied. "We're mostly volunteer, only a couple full-timers. It'll be the state fire marshal's office."

"Page them and the sheriff," Freitas said. "We'll help secure the scene."

"Annie," Parker began, but Freitas shot her a look that stopped her.

The fire had mostly subsided, though it would be hours before it was completely extinguished. Parker went about the business of rolling the crime-scene tape and trying to keep Freitas from tearing up the sheriff's deputies, newly arrived on the scene. Parker tried not to watch as the county medical examiner on call arrived and went about the business of sealing Isabel in a long black bag. Parker kept seeing Isabel and Ryan dancing in front of the fireplace. It had only been an hour or so. It seemed like a dizzy nightmare, a sense of unreality that made everything look strange and impossible. Parker moved in dreamlike automation, feeling disconnected and uncertain.

Freitas kept wandering down to the woods, shining a flashlight borrowed from the firefighters into the darkness between the trees.

A sedan with rolling red lights on the roof pulled up behind the fire trucks and patrol cars.

"I called him," Parker murmured to Chapman's questioning look.

Lieutenant Frank Fradella stepped out of his car and stomped through the snow. Parker pointed around the side of the house and without a word he kept moving. He stumbled a little in the uneven footing, moving through the slush with Parker and Chapman following behind him.

Fradella made it around the back of the house, past the firefighters still tearing into the siding to find hot spots. He walked to where Freitas stood still at the edge of the woods, watching the shadows. Her weapon was drawn but pointed to the ground. Still, he spoke before getting too close.

"Anne," he said, and she turned, her face lit by the flashing red lights from the fire trucks.

"Oh Christ, Frank," Freitas whispered, and he stepped over to her, letting her close. Parker stopped a good distance away, watching as Freitas finally relented, leaning hard on Fradella as he murmured things Parker couldn't hear. It was the first time that Parker realized Freitas was a fairly small woman, shorter than average, as Fradella nearly dwarfed her in his embrace.

Parker leaned backward against Chapman, feeling his solid weight comforting and strong behind her.

Above, the snow began to fall again, blanketing them all in its cold, pale beauty.

Chapter Two

When Dr. Barrington stepped out into the hallway, Parker felt her stomach sink to somewhere around her shoes. She'd been dreading this moment since the sun came up.

"He's waking up," Barrington said.

Parker and Freitas stood up in the dingy, under-lit hallway of Saint Abraham's Hospital, the Memphis facility for vampires. "Is he going to be all right?" Parker asked.

Barrington nodded, peeling off his rubber gloves. "It's a bad concussion but it's healing fast," he said. "If he'd been human, it would probably have killed him. He'll be dizzy for a day or so."

Freitas nodded wordlessly and stepped into the room, Parker behind her.

Ryan drowsed in an iron hospital bed under the flickering fluorescent light. His eyes were half open and unfocused. Then he blinked and seemed to see Parker.

"Ow," he said.

"You took a hell of a knock," Parker said.

Ryan raised a hand to the white bandage on the side of his head. Then sudden fear struck his face. "Isabel? Is she all right?"

Freitas pulled out her notebook in pure cop form, earning her a sharp look from Parker. "What do you remember?"

"Something hit me," Ryan said. "Taking out the trash…someone behind me when I came back up the walk, hit me hard. Then nothing."

"What did he look like?" Freitas pressed.

Abaddon

Ryan stared at her. "I didn't see him, nor am I sure it was a him," he replied. "Detective, what's going on? Where's Isabel? Is she all right?"

Parker looked at Freitas, who lowered her notebook. "There was a fire," Freitas said. "The house burned. It looks like it was set."

Ryan struggled to sit up. "Isabel! Is she okay?"

"I'm sorry to have to tell you, Ryan," Freitas said, her voice unnaturally stiff. "Isabel is dead."

Ryan blinked, staring at Freitas. He seemed to have forgotten Parker was there. Then he started shaking his head back and forth. "That's not possible."

"It's true, Ryan," Parker said quietly, reaching for his hand.

"No, it's not," Ryan muttered, flinging her hand off.

"Ryan, I'm sorry," Parker said, but Ryan's head had fallen back onto the pillows, his eyes closed. "Ryan?"

"Go away," he whispered. "Shut up and go away."

Behind them, Parker heard footsteps. She turned to see Samantha and Danny, pale in the thin morning light, stepping into the room. Samantha was still wearing the light scarf she used to protect herself from the sunlight outside.

"Ryan," Samantha said, her voice full of sadness.

Ryan's eyes shot open and his whole body lurched upward, as though all the cells in his body were screaming at once. He flopped out of the bed and onto the floor, knocking Freitas out of the way. He was wearing only the thin hospital-issue pants and shirt, and the line of his backbone stood out against the fabric as he hunched over as if he had been struck. He let out a moan that turned into something like a scream, his whole body convulsing as he tried to stand and failed, slipping back down onto the floor.

"Ryan!" Danny shouted, moving over to his side. But Ryan flung him off with unnatural strength and Danny stumbled backward into Parker.

Ryan grabbed at the side of the bed, ripping the thin blankets off and flinging them at Freitas, who had retreated to the far corner of the room. His face contorted in fury and misery, sweeping all the detritus off the small table beside his bed. A plastic water pitcher and cup fell to the floor amid fluttering papers.

Samantha stepped between Ryan and the humans. "Ryan," she murmured softly.

Ryan came at her but she deflected his fist and held his arms still between her hands. He staggered again, slipping down into the pile of blankets on the floor. He bucked against her again but she held him firmly, still and calming.

Ryan made a high keening sound in his throat, leaning against Samantha. "Tell me," he whispered, looking up at her.

"It's true," she whispered back.

Ryan buried his head against Samantha. His shoulders were racked with sobs that never quite seemed to make it out into tears but held within, some titanic force of grief that could not be unleashed. His arms shook but the tendons in his forearms stood out in thick cords as he clenched his fists against Samantha's sides.

He whispered something in Samantha's ear and she shook her head violently.

"Please," he begged quietly.

"No," she said, tears flowing down her cheeks. "God, I'm so sorry, Ryan, but no."

Barrington rushed in and, seeing the mess, shot a glare at Parker and Freitas as though holding them responsible. A moment later, two nurses came in to help make up the bed again and Samantha helped Ryan get back into bed. He lay there, passive and blank while Barrington checked the gash on Ryan's head. It was leaking blood again.

Freitas left the room without a word.

Parker leaned over the side of the bed. "We're on this, Ryan," she said forcefully. "Pulling strings, kicking asses. We're going to find out what happened."

Ryan met Parker's eyes and there was a depth of misery in there she could not fathom. She felt it sucking at her, that black chasm inside him, and she had to drop her eyes.

"Everybody out, let my patient rest," Barrington insisted, glaring at Parker.

Samantha started to protest but a look at Ryan's face convinced her. "Rest," she said quietly. "You're not alone."

Ryan stared silently up at the ceiling.

There was no sign of Freitas in the hallway. Parker stopped Samantha and Danny. "I need to talk to you two but first I've got to find Annie," she said. "Will you be at the community center later?"

"All day," Danny said. "How is she doing?"

Parker shrugged. "Who can tell with her? She's tight as a clamshell even when she's not investigating her best friend's murder. It's technically the sheriff's case and they're keeping us in the loop as a professional courtesy. They already talk to you?" Both nodded.

Danny turned to Samantha. "What did Ryan say to you? I couldn't hear."

Samantha lowered her head. "He wanted me to give him the bite."

Parker froze. "Shit."

"Isn't that, you know, fatal for a vampire?" Danny asked.

Samantha nodded, her face miserable. "He was asking me to kill him."

*****

Freitas was sitting in the car with the window rolled down, the December cold riding on the breeze past her face. Parker slipped into the passenger seat and waved the air in front of her nose.

"Damn, what the hell is that?" she asked. "Are you smoking?"

"Yup." Freitas took a deep drag then stubbed the cigarette out in the car's pristine ashtray.

"You don't smoke," Parker said.

Freitas rolled up the window. "I used to. Seemed like a good time to start again."

"Well, I disagree, but let's talk instead about what we're going to do next," Parker said. "Unless you'd like to just walk out of the room again?"

Freitas started the car, turning up the heater. It blew cold air toward them, slowly warming. "I saw what I needed to see. He didn't do it."

Parker gaped at her. "You thought he could have done it?"

Freitas got the car moving. "It's the basics, kid. In a woman's murder, the first suspect is—"

"The man who just proposed to her in front of a roomful of people, who happens to be a friend of yours, who you know adored her," Parker finished. "God, Annie. How did he manage it—get Isabel to sit perfectly still while he bit her then set the fire, which magically waited until he could scamper outside to hit himself over the head with a disappearing tire iron?"

"I saw what I needed to see," Freitas repeated.

"Well, now that we've eliminated the most unlikely suspect, what's next?" Parker snapped.

"Celia," Freitas replied.

Parker choked for a moment or two before answering. "Celia? You're kidding, right?"

"She did one of her trademark disappearing acts at the party, just before everything went to hell," Freitas snapped. "And she's got a record."

"Jesus Christ, Annie, I was just glad they didn't pull her out of that house in a bag!" Parker shouted. "She's a kid!"

Freitas held up her fingers one by one. "Prostitution. Possession—"

"Cannabis, spare me," Parker interjected.

"Aggravated assault—"

"Of her pimp, who fucking deserved it," Parker shot back. "He did a hell of a lot worse to her than she did to him and he got a walk."

"She's got a record, she had opportunity," Freitas said.

"And until the fire marshal comes back with something we can use for means, all that remains is motive," Parker said. "Why the hell would Celia kill Isabel?"

The car pulled into the county building lot. Freitas parked in one of the four County Morgue spaces. "Time for some answers."

* * * * *

Medical examiner Joann Betschart met them at the door and her usual sarcastic cheer was dampened by Freitas' face. "Damn, Annie, I'm so sorry," she began, but Freitas waved her down.

"Just give me the rundown," she said, pulling out the notebook again.

Betschart glanced at Parker, who shook her head. "The sheriff's boys already got my rundown," she said, leading them back into the morgue. "Full tox screen will take a while to get back from the state lab of course, but the cause of death looks like smoke inhalation with exsanguination as a major factor."

In the morgue, a body lay under the center lights, shrouded in a white sheet. Betschart peeled back the sheet, revealing Isabel's unmarked face. Parker flinched and Freitas bit her lip hard enough to draw blood. Betschart glanced at both of them before continuing. She pointed at the side of Isabel's neck.

"Vamp bite, a pretty ugly one," Betschart said. "I'd guess she lost a hell of a lot of blood. Maybe not enough to kill her, if she'd gotten medical assistance pretty quickly. Didn't you say she lived with a vamp?"

"Found outside with a head injury, not a likely suspect," Parker said.

"Well, someone got to her pretty hard," Betschart said. "There was quite a lot of blood on her dress as well, so he didn't drink all of it. Crime scene says there's no way to know how much was at the scene due to the fire and water damage."

"Was—was she awake?" Freitas asked, staring at Isabel's face.

Betschart paused a moment before answering. "Not likely," she said. "She inhaled a lot of smoke so she was breathing. But with the blood loss, she was likely unconscious."

"No ring," Parker said.

Freitas looked at Isabel's left hand. "I'll be damned. Note that, Joann—she's missing a silver claddagh ring with a blue stone."

Betschart wrote on her clipboard. "You're sure she was wearing it at the time?"

"Yes," Parker said, her voice tight.

Freitas reached out and lifted the sheet back over Isabel's face. "Thanks, Joann," she said, and stalked away.

Parker shrugged apologetically and started to follow her. Betschart snagged Parker's jacket sleeve.

"Keep an eye on her," she warned, pitching her voice low. "She's not as tough as she seems. This is personal and she doesn't let things get personal."

Parker gazed after Freitas then back at Isabel's shrouded body. "She doesn't have a choice," she said quietly.

* * * * *

Freitas stepped out of her car and stomped across the snowy yard, crisscrossed with hundreds of tracks. The blackened skeleton of Ryan and Isabel's house was surrounded by yellow crime-scene tape, the snow darkened to a silvery gray with ash and filth.

"Hello!" Freitas called, with Parker following her.

"Stay the hell off the scene!" bellowed a male voice A man wearing a helmet and firefighter's coat stepped into view out of the garage, a disconnected breathing apparatus hanging around his neck. He was at least four inches over six feet and built like a linebacker, light reddish-blond hair escaping from under his cocked helmet.

Freitas held up her shield. "Detective Freitas, this is Detective Parker," she said, indicating her partner. "Whatcha got?"

The investigator came down the driveway toward them. "What I got, I've already given to the sheriff, Detective," he said. "What's your interest here?"

"Sheriff's been keeping us in the loop. We'd appreciate any help you could give us," Freitas said.

The investigator shot her a sharp look. "If they're keeping you in the loop, you can get what you need from them."

Freitas opened her mouth but Parker stepped in. "You know how long it'll take those boys to wind their way through the paperwork," she said. "Meanwhile, this hump's getting away. Give us a break, huh?"

The investigator looked long and hard at Parker before he spoke. "What I've got is a mess of a crime scene, Detectives," he said. "Most of the evidence washed away. In my personal opinion, it's murder-arson, but as far as evidence, I don't have much."

"Shit," Freitas said.

Parker tried for politeness again. "I'm sorry, I didn't get your name."

"Jon Flanigan, state fire marshal's office," he replied, extending a thick-gloved hand. Parker shook with him but Freitas had already wandered off, staring at the charred doorframe. "Something bothering her?" he asked.

Parker pitched her voice low. "The victim was a friend," she said. "I know it's not standard, but if you could give us some idea…"

Flanigan didn't even hesitate this time. "I think it was the simplest form of arson, if you want to make it look like an accident," he said. "Looks like the bug incapacitated the victim in the living room, shut all the doors and laid a trail of papers or trash from the fireplace to the Christmas tree."

"The wrapping paper," Freitas muttered, staring at the cindered doorframe.

"Went up like a torch, filled the room with smoke in less than a minute," Flanigan said.

"Creating a smoke-filled room, not aiming for burning the house," Parker mused.

Flanigan frowned. "Only thing is, there's no way we'd ever call it an accident. The second victim—outside with his head bashed in. If he'd been human, it would've killed him. Plus the neck wound on the fatality."

"Isabel," Freitas snapped. "Her name was Isabel Nelson."

Flanigan inclined his head. "My apologies."

Parker led Flanigan away from Freitas quickly. "So without their injuries…"

"It'd be just another Christmas tragedy," Flanigan said. "Christmas tree set too close to the fireplace. Happens to some family every year. This guy has a brilliantly simple murder plan that we'd never be able to prove and then practically goes out of his way to make sure we don't dismiss it as an accident. He's either a moron or goddamn brilliant."

Parker stared up at what was left of the house. "Anything you can prove in court?"

Flanigan shrugged, taking off his gloves. Wrinkled burn scars traveled up from his fingers to his wrists, disappearing beneath his coat. "No signs of accelerant, most of the evidence washed away, plus with all the damage the firefighters caused by tearing into the structure, there's no way to prove much of this," he said. "We're not gonna catch this bug with forensics. We're gonna catch him the old-fashioned way."

"And what's that?" Freitas snapped.

Flanigan returned her look with a cool gaze of his own. "When he fucks up of course."

* * * * *

The community center stood in the middle of one of Memphis' roughest neighborhoods, an older house dating back to the 1920s that Danny and Samantha had converted with many long afternoons spent hammering and painting, and many more days spent raising money with car washes and nickel drives. Its fenced yard was one of the few on the dilapidated street that still had a scraggly tree, a tire swing suspended by new rope in front of the creaky house. Up the street, glass shattered and voices were raised behind windows that had bars across them.

Across the cracked street rose the beautiful white marble citadel of Saint Bartholomew's Church, a carved monument that had stood in downtown Memphis for more than a century. There were no bars on its windows and surprisingly, no graffiti scrawled on its stone and marble walls.

As Freitas and Parker pulled up, two young girls were walking down the front steps of the community center. They looked no more than fourteen years old but they wore matching vinyl minidresses far too skimpy for the polar wind whipping trash down the street.

"Hey," Parker called, stepping out of the car. The girls glanced up the street as though gauging their chances for getting away. "Relax, I'm not Vice."

The girls turned back toward her. "We're legal," the blonde one said, showing her pointed teeth. Parker's second glance revealed both to be vampires.

"Still, it's goddamn cold," Parker said. "Why not stay in tonight?"

"Gotta work," the other girl said. Unlike the first one, her blonde hair was an obviously cheap bottle job with dark roots showing at her crown.

Parker pulled out her wallet and handed them a pair of twenties. "Take the night off."

The blonde shoved the money back at her, to the incredulous stare of her friend. "We don't need your money," she said harshly. "We earn our living."

"Call it payment for information," Parker said. "Anything you can tell me about that group of vamps who went missing?"

The bottle-blonde laughed. "Please. The number of times you cops ask us about that shit...man, that was months ago. Those guys are in Costa Rica or some shit."

Parker shrugged. "They killed four cops. We take that personal." She shoved the twenties and her business card back at them. "Consider it a down payment. You hear anything about them, gimme a call."

This time they took the money. As they vanished down the street, Freitas stepped up onto the sidewalk, pulling a long drag on her cigarette. "How much money have you paid out to the pros since Diego's escape?" she asked.

Parker fanned the air in front of her face dramatically. "I can still pay my rent."

"They're right, Diego and his henchvamps are long gone," Freitas said. "He ever shows up in the U.S. again, it's an automatic death sentence. Times four. He shows up in Memphis again and he won't get the chance to plead insanity. Chris Cox will gun him the fuck down in the street."

"And any vamp he happens to see," Parker said, trudging up the neatly shoveled walkway. "That guy is as crazy as Diego."

"Don't confuse crazy with extreme dedication," Freitas said. "He was never fond of the vamps to begin with, and that was before Diego ate four of his men."

"Yeah, well, he's the wrong guy to head up the Chain Gang," Parker returned. "His goons are beating up any vamp they see on the slightest offense."

"You know that?" Freitas asked. "You have witnesses, signed statements?"

"Um..."

"Yeah." Freitas stubbed out her cigarette on the sole of her boot. They entered the community center where a cheerful fire was blazing in the fireplace. A couple of Hispanic teenagers were playing ping-pong in the corner while three black girls chatted on the couch, half listening to the TV in the corner.

Parker nearly bumped into a man on his way out the door, pulling on his black coat. "Forgive me, Father," she said, smiling.

"You have not sinned," said the priest, smiling back. "At least not lately."

"Now, Father, I've been pretty good," Parker returned. "Father, have you met my partner? Detective Anne Freitas, meet Father Patrick Stubblefield, dean of Saint Bartholomew's."

Freitas shook his hand with as much grace as she was capable.

"Father Stubblefield was one of the first to support the community center and his parishioners often volunteer here," Parker said.

"We only help what Samantha and Danny created," Stubblefield said. "They have brought hope and life to this neighborhood in ways we would never have imagined a few years ago. They are truly doing God's work."

"I though the church frowned on vampires," Freitas said. Parker shot her a look.

"Officially, the church may decry a particular practice or lifestyle, but we never condemn the person," Stubblefield said. "Our doors are always open. We have many years of shameful history to overcome and I can think of no better way than to serve God's people of all color, creed and race."

"My apologies, Father. Most men of the cloth I've met haven't been quite so…open-minded," Freitas said.

"No apology necessary," Father Stubblefield said. "Now if you'll excuse me, I'm going to try to visit Ryan at Saint Abraham's."

Parker blinked. "You know Ryan Callahan?"

"Well, he volunteered here from time to time," Father Stubblefield said. "He and Isabel had spoken with me a few times about attending services and I assured them they would be welcome. They hadn't chosen to do so but I imagine if there was ever a time when a man needed a spiritual counselor… At any rate, he may tell me to, pardon the expression, go to hell. But I'll try."

Abaddon

"Good luck, Father," Parker said, and waved as the priest stepped out into the cold.

"What did he mean about shameful history?" Freitas asked.

"Maybe just the persecution of vampires by the church?" Parker mused.

"He means the riots," said a boy lounging by the fireplace. Lucas was about eighteen, a darkly handsome boy still growing into his height. Celia was curled up next to him on the floor in front of the fireplace and Parker breathed a silent thanks that she was here and apparently all right. She didn't care for how closely Celia was snuggling with Lucas, but as much time as they'd been spending together, she figured it was to be expected.

"Nice to see you," Parker said sarcastically. Celia ignored her, draping her arm around Lucas' thin shoulders.

"In the 1870s, there were riots all around here," Lucas said. "They thought vampires carried yellow fever or something. They burned out the vamp shanties, killed a lot of vamps. Even then this neighborhood was a shithole."

"Language," Freitas corrected automatically.

"How do you know this stuff?" Parker asked.

Lucas shrugged. "It was on the local history test last week," he said. "Some of us study."

"Hey!" Celia said, poking him in the side. Lucas grinned at her.

Samantha stuck her head into the rec room. "Somebody close the door! It's December!" She saw Freitas and Parker and her face changed. "Come on in," she said more quietly, and they followed her past the staring teenagers into the small office.

Samantha dropped into the chair behind her desk, a framed photo of herself with Danny smiling up at them. "God, what a rotten day," she said. "How are you two doing?"

"Just peachy," Parker said, sitting down. Freitas remained standing. "Things going okay here?"

"There were a couple of girls here who knew Isabel from her volunteer work here," Samantha said. "I had to hold a few hands. The hospital wouldn't let me back in to see Ryan. He's on suicide watch."

"How did Celia take it?" Freitas asked, and Parker shot her a glare.

Samantha hesitated. "She already knew," she said. "Told me she heard it on the street. Celia's pretty well locked up, it's really hard to tell how she's feeling. As you know."

Freitas was scribbling in her notebook and Parker decided to ignore her. "Where's Danny?" she asked.

Samantha shook her head. "Upstairs, yelling at Children's Services again. Trying to get a kid pulled out of what we know is a fireweed den but nobody busts it."

Parker blinked. "How come I don't know about this?"

Samantha smiled sadly. "You want my whole list of things I'd like fixed in this neighborhood?"

"No, but I'll take the fireweed den," Parker said.

Samantha closed her eyes. "I still can't quite believe it," she said. "God, poor Ryan."

"Tell me about it," Danny said, coming into the office from behind Freitas. "Children's Services is moving it up to priority two, hon."

"Thanks for small favors," Samantha groused.

Danny clicked on the small television in the corner. "Here it comes."

The TV clicked onto the local newscast. A few moments of inane chatter from the blow-dried anchors switched to reporter Dana Franks, her red hair blown about by the wind as she stood in front of Ryan and Isabel's burned-out home. "A woman was killed early this morning when her home, located just outside the city limits, caught fire," Franks said. "Isabel

Nelson, age twenty-six, was declared dead at the scene after county firefighters pulled her from the home, which caught fire shortly after a Christmas party had ended at the house. Ms. Nelson's live-in boyfriend, a vampire, sustained minor injuries and is listed in stable condition at Saint Abraham's Hospital. Authorities are listing the fire as suspicious in nature but have declined to discuss any details. For Channel 13, I'm Dana Franks."

The screen switched back to the faux-sorrowful anchor, who immediately switched gears to ask an unseen person about the weather. Danny switched off the TV with a bit more force than was necessary. "That's it? 'Suspicious', and that's all?"

"The sheriff likely withheld certain salient facts," Parker explained. "You don't want reporters buzzing around and mucking up your evidence."

"And if it had been a vampire woman killed instead of a human? How much press would it have gotten then?" Danny snapped.

"Easy, hon," Samantha said. "Kelly and Anne don't make the news."

"Sorry, it just pisses me off," Danny said, still mostly talking to Parker. "Isabel deserved a better send-off than to be a footnote before the weather report."

Parker nodded. "Dana Franks is the only reporter who even did a story. The rest shrugged."

Samantha rubbed her face with her hands. "I still can't quite believe it," she said again. "It's like something I keep tripping over in my mind that just doesn't quite fit. How can Isabel be gone? And right after..."

"I know," Freitas said sharply.

"I'm sorry, Anne," Samantha said to the detective. "I know how close you two were. This has got to be terrible for you."

"I'll let it be terrible after I find out who did it," Freitas said coldly. "That's why I'm here."

Samantha froze for a moment, sudden comprehension dawning on her face. "Diego."

Danny immediately moved over beside Samantha, reflexively protective. "Dear Christ, you think he's behind this?"

"There's no shortage of lunatics in this town," Freitas said. "But only one has gotten away from us lately. As I recall, you've got some kind of link to Diego and if he's been lurking around lately, you might know it."

Parker glared at her partner. "So all that talk about him being in Timbuktu?"

"Covering the bases, kid," Freitas said without taking her eyes off Samantha. "Well?"

Samantha shook her head. "It's not like I can close my eyes and dial his number," she said. "He didn't complete the kiss to bind me to him. The most I'd ever get is a shadow of him."

"Any shadows lately?" Freitas pressed.

Samantha frowned, a look of concentration on her face. She shook her head but her eyes were troubled.

"Hon?" Danny asked. "I know there was a moment during the party…"

"It was nothing," Samantha insisted to Parker and Freitas' interested faces. "I did sense something, just for a moment, but it was my imagination. Something familiar…but not Diego," she added hastily. "Believe me, if I ever sense Diego again, you two are on my speed dial. And you should bring all the guns and chains you can muster."

"Don't have to tell me twice," Parker said, lightly touching a faint scar on her neck.

Freitas snapped the notebook closed. "There's a few more rocks to kick over. But you sense anything, hear from anyone…"

"Speed dial," Danny promised. "We've had enough of death and mystery, believe me."

As if in response, both Parker's and Freitas' cell phones went off in unison, signaling text messages. They glanced at them and Parker was on her feet in a moment.

"What is it?" Danny asked.

Freitas was already out the door. Parker paused long enough to respond over her shoulder. "Another fire."

* * * * *

The stately suburban house was already fully engulfed in flames when Freitas and Parker pulled up in front, smoking curling between the white pillars and obscuring the front door. Flanigan was just ahead of them, climbing out of his car and hanging up his cell phone while the firefighters trained their hoses on the house.

"They get her out?" Freitas yelled, hurrying up to him.

Flanigan shook his head. "What they got out didn't live long," he said, pointing to the ambulance. "No question about it—something did a real number on her. She didn't get the chance to inhale smoke—EMTs said the perp ripped her goddamn throat out."

"Thanks for the call," Parker said, and Flanigan nodded to her.

"What about him?" Freitas asked.

"Might still be in the house, in which case he's dead as hell," Flanigan said, staring at the flames as they roared out the shattered windows. Blackened shingles fell off the roof as the powerful hose stream struck it, sending clouds of steam billowing up with the smoke into the sky. "They couldn't risk sending in another team. Too dangerous."

Freitas shook her head. "He's not in there," she said. "This hump, he doesn't kill the guy."

"That's assuming it's the same guy. Could be a coincidence," Flanigan said.

Freitas leveled her stare at him. "Do you believe in coincidences?"

Flanigan stared right back. "Nope," he said.

"Besides, he damn near killed Ryan," Parker pointed out.

"But didn't," Freitas returned. "The perp had him knocked out, he could've cut his head off. Instead he left Ryan alive, outside where we'd find him."

"Then let's search, before the rest of my evidence gets washed away," Flanigan said. He stepped over and spoke to the scene commander for a moment. Then he signaled for Freitas and Parker to follow him.

They moved around the back of the house where more firefighters aimed hoses at the house and shouted to each other. Careful to stay out of their way, Freitas and Parker followed Flanigan in a wide berth to the backyard. The snow was now slushy and gray close to the house, white and unbroken farther away toward the alley that provided access behind the row of stately homes.

Except for the footprints. "Shit!" Parker said. "Flanigan, freeze where you are!"

Flanigan stopped moving instantly and Parker pulled out her cell phone again and snapped pictures. "Same retreat, escaping out the back while EMS arrives in front," she said.

A section of the roof fell in, sending a shout of flame into the sky.

Flanigan led them back around the other side, past the garage, silent and dark. It was connected to the main house only by a glass corridor lined with plants. The glass was now cracked and smoky, the plants inside crisped in their pots.

They came back around the garage to the wide driveway where the ambulance was parked. Freitas and Parker took a quick look inside and mercifully all they saw was the zipped-up black bag.

Behind them, two media vans rolled up. "Shit," Parker said.

"Yeah, that's to be expected," Freitas said with a harsh zing of bitterness to her voice. "He's an important man. More important than Isabel."

Another car pulled up and Lieutenant Chris Cox stepped out, raising his collar against the cold.

"Shit, it's the Chain Gang," Parker muttered. "They figured out the connection."

"He's an asshole, not an idiot," Freitas reminded her. "Besides, it's just Cox, not the whole Chain Gang."

"Chain Gang?" Flanigan asked.

"They use silver chains to restrain arrested vampires," Parker said. "Vampires are allergic to silver so it feels like acid on the skin. Keeps them from trying to break the chains. At least six lawsuits have tried to argue that it's cruel and unusual punishment, especially since they haven't yet been found guilty of anything, but the protests keep getting shot down."

"Bet we'd be happy to have the silver chains if Diego were in town," Freitas said.

"Didn't work last time," Parker returned. "Besides, I'd rather have a howitzer in hand if Diego comes to town."

"Do I get to hear who Diego is?" Flanigan wondered.

"Later," Parker promised.

Cox strode up the driveway. "I'll be damned, if it ain't the Bobbsey Twins," he chortled. "Scoping for more work, Freitas?"

"Personal interest," Freitas said coolly.

Cox surveyed the scene. "Sorry to hear about your friend," he said, his voice completely neutral.

"Thanks," Freitas replied tonelessly.

"You're not mucking up my scene, are you?" Cox asked Flanigan, essentially dismissing Parker completely.

"My scene," Flanigan said, holding up his badge. "Jon Flanigan, state fire marshal's office."

"Our scene then," Cox amended. "Sheriff's boys turned it over to me as soon as they heard about this. They were still thinking it might be a freak accident."

"Idiots," Flanigan muttered then changed his tone when he saw Cox's face. "No offense, Lieutenant. Just that I told them about nineteen times that there is no way to tear your own throat out or hit yourself over the head with a weapon that vanishes while you're unconscious. By accident."

Cox shrugged. "Between you, me and the girls here, a lot of 'em are idiots," he said. "Just weren't interested if it was vamps."

"And you are?" Parker asked.

Cox turned his glare on her. "I hope you're not thinking of going on one of your leech-loving crusades, girl," he said.

"That's 'Detective Parker', Cox, and we're just trying to find the fucker," Freitas snapped, before Parker could say something stupid or hit Cox over the head with the nearest blunt object.

"If you don't mind, I've got a job to do," Cox said. "Try to stay out of my way." He wandered over to the scene commander and Flanigan followed.

"I hate that fucker," Parker fumed. "And if he calls me 'girl' again, I may just…"

"Get used to it, it doesn't stop when you pass thirty," Freitas said absently. Flanigan was shouting at the scene commander, looking frustrated. Cox looked bored. The scene commander shook his head and continued ignoring Flanigan.

Flanigan turned back to them, fury on his face. "Dammit, that's standard procedure," he said, stumping up the driveway. "Nobody's bothered to search the fucking garage yet."

Freitas started to follow him and Flanigan held up his hand. "Stay back," he warned.

"The fire's in the house, the garage isn't affected!" Freitas shouted.

"You know that? When did you go to the academy?" Flanigan shouted back.

"Shut up! We're coming," Parker said, and Flanigan turned to her. "If the roof falls in, we'll run," she amended, and Flanigan rolled his eyes before going back up the driveway.

They followed him into the darkened garage, holding up their flashlights at eye level. Freitas moved around to the side of the black sedan parked in the center of the garage.

"Shit, we gotta get that out of here before the heat does something combustible to it," Flanigan muttered, looking under the car.

Tools hung neatly on the walls and the trash-can lids were set on the cans. The flickering yellow light from the burning house shone through the small garage window, casting an eldritch glow to compete with the steady beam of Flanigan's flashlight and the flashing lights from the emergency vehicles out front.

"Freitas," Parker said, motioning toward the car.

Freitas moved over beside her. There were long scratches on the trunk lid. "Maybe someone keyed his car," she murmured.

"Yeah, and the guy meticulous enough to hang up his goddamn snow shovel is gonna just drive it around like that," Parker said.

Freitas glanced at her partner. "Smart kid."

Parker rolled her eyes and unholstered her gun. Flanigan quietly opened the driver's side door. "Ready?" he asked.

Freitas pulled her own gun, keeping it pointed safely at the ground. "Ready."

Flanigan popped the lid, and it slipped open but didn't rise. Parker lifted her booted foot with the characteristic grace of the long-trained martial artist she was and nudged it into the air.

Drew Sanford lay in the trunk of his own car, blood staining the immaculate carpet under his head.

"Medic!" Parker shouted, and Flanigan dropped his flashlight in his rush past Parker to the man in the trunk.

"Careful, Flanigan!" Freitas warned. Her gun was still out.

"Jesus, Annie, give it a rest," Parker said, holstering her gun. "Do we move him?"

"Help me," Flanigan said, sliding his hands under the vampire's weight. Parker supported Sanford's head and shoulders while Flanigan bore the brunt of the weight. Freitas stepped out into the bright lights to shout again for a paramedic.

Parker laid Sanford out on the ground. She automatically tried to take his pulse then smacked herself on the head for an idiot. Flanigan shone his flashlight into Sanford's unresponsive eyes.

"Shit, is he dead?" Parker asked.

"How do you tell?" Flanigan muttered.

Sanford's hand snapped up and grabbed Flanigan's wrist. The flashlight dropped to the garage floor and went out.

"Easy, Mr. Sanford," Parker said, trying to disengage his grip on Flanigan's wrist. It was a white-knuckled death grip, had to hurt like hell, but Flanigan only tightened his jaw.

Sanford's eyes slowly cleared, focusing on Parker and Flanigan. "Beth," he whispered. "Beth…is in the house."

Parker glanced over at Flanigan, whose eyes mirrored hers in sudden empathy. "I'm sorry, Mr. Sanford—" she began. But before she could say any more, Sanford pushed up to a sitting position. Flanigan tried to restrain him but Sanford shoved him away. He stood up, a bit unsteady.

Above them, something struck the garage roof with a thunderous drumming.

"Gotta get out of here," Flanigan said, helping Sanford stumble out of the garage, blood still dripping down the side of the vampire's head.

The fire had nearly consumed the brick home, the pillars blackened and smoking. The roof was falling in as firefighters trained their hoses on nearby trees, the garage roof and the wall nearest the next home to keep it from spreading. The orange glow rose into the sky, reflecting onto the billowing mushroom cloud of smoke. Small bits of debris, glowing bright in the flames, floated high on the rising hot air and vanished into the darkness.

Sanford stood on his own lawn and the light of the flames danced in his blank eyes. On the other side of the property, Freitas was returning with a pair of paramedics.

"She's not in there!" Flanigan shouted to Sanford, over the roar of the hoses and shouts of the firefighters.

Sanford didn't seem to hear him. He just stood there in the firelight, and when his body sagged again, Parker and Flanigan were there to catch him.

Chapter Three

"Investigation of the case has been turned over to the Parahuman Task Force, under the command of Lieutenant Chris Cox with the Memphis Police Department," said Dana Franks, standing in front of the burned-out husk of the Sanford home. "Beth Sanford was declared dead at the scene, and although authorities would not give specifics, they said it likely that she would have died even if the house hadn't gone up in flames. The fire is being investigated as suspicious in nature and officials said they have strong evidence to believe it was arson.

"The home's owner, Drew Sanford, is the founder of Vampires Against Mortal Perversion, a conservative vampire group that has pushed to make vampire prostitution and selling of vampire bites illegal. VAMP has come under attack from its own constituency as vampires have argued removing the bite and sex trades will make it nearly impossible for vampires to make a legal living while they are restricted from so many other occupations. And of course VAMP has often been the target of protests from anti-vampire groups as well. Sanford himself has gained some stature in recent years and his endorsement has been sought by political candidates and vampire rights groups alike.

"But today the VAMP office bears a funeral wreath and a recorded message informs us that the office is closed to allow workers to mourn for Beth Sanford, the group's treasurer and life partner of its founder. Drew Sanford is listed in stable condition at Saint Abraham's Hospital, which informs us he will see no visitors except law enforcement personnel."

Abaddon

Dana Franks paused, and for a moment Samantha thought she was just going to stop as the polar wind blew through her short red hair. But then Dana began speaking again and the camera wavered a bit, as though she were going off script.

"This is the second death in a suspicious fire in days and both involved vampire-human couples," she went on. "Isabel Nelson, a human, died in a suspicious fire Tuesday night at her town just outside the city limits, leaving her live-in boyfriend, vampire Ryan Callahan, seriously injured. Police would not say whether they believe the two incidents are related."

The camera cut quickly to the blow-dried anchorman. "Dana, we understand there have been several public statements made?"

The camera switched back to Dana. "Yes, Jim. Congressman Joe Renfrow has offered his condolences in a statement and the mayor has said all the city's resources will be placed at the fire marshal's disposal to find the culprit."

"Sure they will," Samantha muttered as the news moved on to last-minute shoppers at the mall. "For a week."

"Well, be fair, Samantha," said Robert Carton, sitting on the couch in Danny's living room. "If they don't catch them in a week, they're not likely to catch them at all. That's just the way it is with police work."

"And I'm sure they're really putting all their resources at the fire marshal's disposal," Danny snarked from the kitchen where he was pulling something out of the oven.

"Sure they are, now that it's Drew Sanford," Samantha groused. "They love him. He's a stand-up vampire, never asks for more than they want to give."

"Hey, I was impressed with some of his thoughts on stopping Tunstall's Law," Robert said.

"Dad, anyone with a brain was against Tunstall's Law and it was that idiot Renfrow who got it pushed through,"

Danny called from the kitchen. "He even wanted it expanded to schools so vampires couldn't be teachers as well as firefighters, cops or work in hospitals. The sheer loss from the workforce…"

"I don't know about that," Samantha said unhappily. "Not so many vamps are working in those jobs now."

"Openly," Danny countered. "I bet there's a lot of closet vamps."

Samantha snorted. "It's not easy to stay closeted for long. Trust me, I know."

"Fooled us long enough," Robert countered, smiling at her.

Samantha smiled back. "It's all Danny's fault," she said, glossing over the slight discomfort this subject brought. It was always strange to have dinner with Danny's father, though unavoidable as she remained a part of Danny's life. It had been difficult to set aside seeing Robert in the dark rooms of Nocturnal Urges, a secret client when she was selling the bite to random strangers for a paycheck. Even more uncomfortable was the knowledge that he had been opposed to her relationship with Danny from the beginning, fearing the prejudice and hatred they would face—and some part of her, some practical kernel that did not concern itself with love, still felt Robert might be right in the end.

But then Danny stepped into the room with a plateful of cinnamon chocolate-chip cookies varying from massive, barely cooked monsters to tiny briquettes the size of silver dollars, and she couldn't help but smile at his proud face.

Robert smiled. "Danny, what did you do?"

Danny glanced down at the cookies. "Okay, so they're a little…uneven."

Samantha took a medium-sized one and smiled. "They'll taste just fine."

Robert shook his head. "You let him cook?"

"Sometimes I'm brave," Samantha returned.

"I'm a better cook than she is," Danny said, relaxing into a chair. "You'd think in a hundred years, she'd learn something other than crab cakes."

"I was busy," Samantha said, smiling. "Besides, you like my crab cakes."

Danny grinned at her and she sensed him thinking something quite lascivious. *Don't you dare say that,* she whispered, and she felt a flutter of amusement from him. The link they shared was tenuous but constant, forged in the bond between human and vampire and reinforced the longer they were together. Being human, he could not consciously communicate with her—at least not yet—but Samantha's mental skills were strong and she could often read his emotions at a distance.

Robert clicked off the TV, his face turning serious. "I am so sorry about your friend," he told Samantha. "Is there anything we can do for her...partner?" His voice faltered at the end, as though he weren't quite sure of the word to use.

"Partner is appropriate," she told him. "Though it's closer to wife, sort of. Ryan asked her to be his consort at the party, right before..." Her own voice trailed off.

"Yeah, you have to explain that to me," Danny said quickly. "What's a consort?"

"Technically, it's the closest thing we have to marriage, since the law won't recognize vamp-human marriage," Samantha said. "It started with the vampire kiss, when several vampires are bound to a single master vampire, under his control. The consort is his favorite, who essentially serves as his second-in-command, though she has no real authority."

"Is the master always a man?" Robert asked.

Samantha shook her head. "I've never met a female master, but I've heard of them. A master vampire must have immense mental control and experience. He or she has to be able to keep control of the kiss at all times and so it helps to have a consort with great strength to complement his. Her power sort of lends itself to him, like a battery backup," she said, struggling to find an analogy that they would understand. "Since the tradition of the kiss has mostly fallen away, the term 'consort' is sort of a formal way of asking someone to be your life partner, a commitment as close to marriage as we are allowed. It's a serious commitment, one not taken easily. After all, humans only have one life to share."

Robert grinned. "So you two..."

"Not yet," Danny said, winking at Samantha. "Someone's feet are a little chilly."

"Let's just go six more months without psycho vampires popping out of the woodwork and we'll talk," Samantha said.

Danny pretended to check his watch. "So that's when you'll move in with me?"

"Don't start," Samantha said, her tone light.

"Don't tell me you're still living at the community center!" Robert protested.

Danny shook his head. "I keep telling her she's out of her mind. Perfectly nice house I have here, safe neighborhood..."

"A singing robotic fish in the rec room," Samantha chided.

Danny clapped his hand over his heart. "I would give up my singing robotic fish for you, Samantha."

Robert chortled and Samantha smiled at Danny. "Six more months," she repeated. "Now, I'm afraid it's time for me to turn into a pumpkin."

Danny's face fell. *Stay,* she heard him think, and she shook her head slightly as she rose to her feet, looking around for her coat. "I've got to be at the community center early in the morning. I'll see you two at dinner tomorrow? Seven o'clock at the center?"

Robert stood immediately and helped her get her coat on. "Good night, Samantha," he said kindly.

Abaddon

Danny walked with her to the door and once they were outside in the chilly air, he took her hand in his. "You only need to say the word and you never have to drive home in the cold again," he said.

Samantha squeezed his hand. "I know."

Danny slid an arm around her shoulders, as though trying to keep her close. "Can I get a real reason this time? Then I promise to shut up about it for five whole days."

Samantha smiled at him but her heart was chilled by more than the cold. Unbidden, the memory rose in her mind of Todd lying in that long-ago Chicago alley. Todd, a young police officer who drifted in her path what seemed like centuries ago, but was only a few decades in the past. More boy than man, a lover who had meant no harm and was murdered for the sin of loving her and wanting her with him.

She felt Danny trying in his clumsy human way to sense her through their link and she hid it behind a quick wall. But not quickly enough.

"Whoa," he said, blinking at her. "I must be getting better at this... Why am I seeing a policeman's badge?"

"I was thinking of Anne and Kelly," she lied, and hated herself for it immediately, especially since he must sense the lie through the link like a yellow green flare. "How they're coming along on the fire investigation."

"Is that what you're really doing tomorrow? Talking to Anne and Kelly? Because the center's closed," Danny said, and now there was a slight edge to his voice.

"I'm going to pick up Ryan at Saint Abraham's," Samantha said. "I'm sorry, I just felt weird talking about it in front of your father."

"Okay, I don't get why, but that's no big deal," Danny said. "I should go with you. To pick up Ryan."

Samantha shook her head. "He's not in any fit state, they shouldn't even be letting him out," she said.

Danny frowned. "I know he's your friend more than mine, Samantha. But I want to help too. And you shouldn't have to go through that alone."

Samantha smiled at him, at his earnest face filled with such concern. "You always want to save the world," she said softly, touching the side of his face. "But you can't help him. It's…"

"A vampire thing? I wouldn't understand?" Danny said, and there was a touch more harshness in his voice than she liked to hear.

"Oh good Lord, you are not jealous," Samantha said, incredulous. "Of Ryan? Of all people?"

Danny flushed a little. "Sometimes it's a bit creepy that you've got a window in my head," he said. "I'm just an ordinary human male, full of flaws, you'll have to excuse me."

"Ryan is not… I mean…" Unbidden, she saw the image in Danny's mind, an image from her memories that had apparently been bothering him for a while. An image of her and Ryan, entwined in passionate embrace, his mouth pressed against the swells of her breasts above her tightly laced bodice.

Samantha burst out laughing. She couldn't help it. "Daniel Robert Carton, that was *work*," she said. "Playacting for the marks. Four years ago, before he became assistant manager. Good heavens, you are the silliest man." She reached up and kissed Danny thoroughly on the mouth. "But you are *my* man."

Danny smiled against her mouth and she sensed a tiny flood of relief from him. She couldn't help giggling again. But another image from Danny shot through to her, of Ryan on the floor of the hospital room, entwined in the sheets, shuddering against Samantha's shoulder. It cut through her giggles like a sudden frost, freezing any good humor out of the evening.

"I'm not jealous of Ryan," Danny said softly into her ear. "Not really. God, I can't imagine if something happened to you again, not again…"

Abaddon

She caught another glimpse then—of Danny by his mother's coffin, sprinkling yellow rose petals on the shining wood, interposed with the image of Samantha on a hospital gurney, blood covering her chest, fading away before his eyes.

"Oh Danny," she murmured, holding him close to her, comforting him in her arms. "Nothing's going to happen to me."

"You don't know that," he said, his voice rough. "Ryan, now this poor Sanford guy, they're vampires and they couldn't stop it and now…"

"Shh," she said, kissing him again. "It's okay. It'll all be okay."

Danny nodded but in his mind she heard him think, *Not for Ryan.*

"No," she said with sorrow. "Not for Ryan."

* * * * *

The chill wind blew through the parking lot. Parker stamped her feet and wished she could get into the car with Freitas already. The car hummed behind her as Freitas waited for her.

"I just wanted to make sure you were doing okay," Chapman said, studying her in that intense way he had. Everything with Chapman was intense. Even when he was playful, there always seemed to be something behind it.

"Not really," Parker sighed. "Annie's worse."

Chapman shook his head. "I never thought you two would be able to keep working together."

"I like a challenge," Parker said with a ghost of a smile. "Listen, she's really chomping at the bit. We've got to go."

"You two are gonna step on Cox's toes again," Chapman said. There was an odd neutrality to his tone that bothered her.

"Cox can kiss my ass," Parker said, but there was little heat behind it. She was tired, heartsick and not entirely sure why Chapman wanted to talk to her right at this second.

Chapman looked down at his uniform shoes, seemingly uncomfortable.

"What? What is it?" Parker asked. "Hey, Michael. What's the deal?"

"My promotion's going through," Chapman said, not looking at her.

Parker blinked. "That's great! And totally overdue, you're way too good a cop to stay an officer," she said, reaching out to his arm. If he'd been looking at her, she might have hugged him. "What's wrong? You don't seem happy about it. Isn't this what you wanted, to get off the shit detail?"

He looked up at her. "It's conditional, and you're not gonna like the condition."

Parker frowned. "Conditional? They can't still be pissed about—"

"They are," Chapman said, cutting her off. "I'm a sergeant effective at the new year, if I accept transfer to the Parahuman Task Force."

Parker gaped. "The Chain Gang?"

"I know how you feel about them," Chapman said in a rush. "I know what you think of them. But there's good work to be done in parahuman police work and if good people get involved…"

"Good people can get chewed up into pieces by Cox and his fucking goons!" Parker snapped. "Cox is on a mission to burn out all the vampires in the city! The Chain Gang is a legalized form of the Ku Klux Klan, how can you even think about being a part of—"

"How can I not, Kelly!" Chapman shouted back. "I'm stuck a fucking officer long after everyone my age has moved up. You're a detective, for God's sake, you used to be my partner!"

Parker's eyes flashed. "You know I passed the exam ungodly early. I'm still not convinced there wasn't a computer error," she snapped. "If this is some kind of bullshit ego thing to prove—"

"It's not ego, it's not bullshit, I'm tired of writing tickets and scraping drunks off the road at two a.m. on a Saturday night," Chapman snapped. "If I'm with the Chain Gang, I can get involved with real, ongoing cases that involve more of my brain than running plates."

Parker folded her arms. "So what happens when Cox tells you to go find a vamp and beat the shit out of him for some meaningless piece of info?" she asked.

"That won't happen," Chapman said, but he dropped his eyes.

"The hell it won't," Parker cried. "You just don't care! What? Aren't 'parahumans' human enough for you anymore? You starting to believe Cox's bullshit about the secret plan to overthrow the human race? Jesus, Michael, how stupid are you?"

"Fuck you!" Chapman shouted. Parker heard Freitas open her car door behind her but didn't turn around. She was too angry.

"They were my friends too, Kelly!" Chapman yelled. "You know I goddamn-well care and I'm not going to turn into a fucking monster just because I'm working with someone who may be a monster!"

"Officer, your voice is carrying," Freitas said quietly, standing right behind Parker.

Chapman didn't seem to notice Freitas. His eyes bored into Parker's. "I knew it would be like this," he said, the anger still strong in his voice even though he had stopped shouting. "You expect the worst of me, of everyone. You have no faith in me, Kelly. You never have."

"That's bullshit," Parker snapped, but Chapman was already turning away as she spoke. "Michael!"

Chapman kept walking. Parker took a step toward him but then she faltered. His form grew smaller as he crossed the parking lot, heading toward the station house.

Freitas spoke quietly. "If you've got stuff to do, we can do this later," she said.

"No," Parker said, staring after Chapman as he went into the station house without looking back. "No, I'm good."

"You sure?" Freitas asked.

Parker turned, her face impassive. "Yeah. Let's do this thing."

They got back into the car and Freitas immediately lit up a cigarette. Parker rolled down the car window, her mute protest at the cloud of smoke that now filled the car.

"Shut that window, it's December," Freitas said.

Parker fanned the air dramatically in front of her face and Freitas stubbed out the cigarette. "Happy?"

"Ecstatic," Parker grumbled. "Do you plan to tell me where we're going? I thought we were going to hammer on that anti-vamp protester guy."

"Osborne's off the hook," Freitas said. "He's doing three months."

Parker blinked. "You're kidding."

"It was his ninth trespass and his people have gotten really pushy at their protests. Nothing violent yet but they threw the book at him." Freitas changed lanes toward an off-ramp near the airport.

"Then where the hell are we going?" Parker asked. "Don't we have a long list of vamp haters we could be annoying right now?"

"Chris Cox is doing that," Freitas said neutrally.

"Motherfuck," Parker said, staring out the window. "Like Cox gives a good goddamn about human-vamp couples getting killed."

"He knows the vamp world and he's relentless," Freitas said.

"He's a psycho bigot and he's gonna step over the line one day," Parker said with heat. "So if he's beating up the hate groups, where are we going?"

Freitas pulled into a parking lot by a large office building. "I know somebody Cox wouldn't think of," she said.

Parker followed Freitas into the building, standing resolute as Freitas flashed her badge at security and was directed to the information systems department. When they reached a sea of cubicles, Freitas marched directly to a handsome young man with sandy-brown hair who was just hanging up the phone.

"Duane Russell," Freitas said. "You might not remember me. Detective Freitas, and this is my partner Detective Kelly Parker."

Russell blinked at them. "I sure as hell remember you," he said, and the hostility in his voice immediately put Parker on guard.

"Somewhere we can talk?" Freitas asked.

Russell stood and clearly thought twice before gesturing toward an empty conference room. A few heads poked out of cubicles but none seemed more than curious.

In the conference room, Parker stood behind Freitas, ready to back up whatever game Freitas was playing.

"When was the last time you talked to Isabel Nelson?" Freitas asked.

Russell rolled his eyes. "What the hell, that was a long time ago," he said.

"When did you last see her?" Freitas pressed.

Russell thought for a second. "I saw her here at work from time to time but I kind of avoided her department, okay?" he said. "Maybe two months, just passing in the hall. Last time I spoke with her was the day, you know…"

"The day we caught Elyse Callahan," Freitas said. "Haven't talked to Isabel since then? What about Ryan?"

"Just the inquest," Russell said. "But we didn't really speak then either—they kept me outside then said my testimony wasn't necessary. What the hell is going on, Detective?"

"Where were you two nights ago?" Parker asked.

"What the fuck!" Russell exploded. "I was home with my girlfriend and I'm done answering anything until you tell me what's going on!"

"Isabel is dead," Freitas said flatly. "Looks like she was murdered."

Russell seemed taken aback. He stepped back from Freitas as if she had physically reached out to hit him.

"Guess you don't watch the news," Parker said.

Russell leaned hard on one of the office chairs around the gleaming conference table. "For sure? She's really…"

"Yes," Freitas said. "Her house was set on fire with her inside."

Russell stared down at the conference table for a moment. When he spoke again, the anger was gone from his voice. "I see why you came to me," he said, his head still down. "Makes sense. I admit it, I didn't take it well when she left me."

"Got yourself kicked out of Nocturnal Urges one too many times, from what I hear," Freitas said.

The name of the club acted like a shot of adrenaline on him as his head snapped up. "Fuckin' leeches," Russell snarled. "You look at the one she was shacked up with? Did he go nuts again and suck her dry?"

"Wasn't him," Parker said coolly. "He got hurt too."

"I'm crying," Russell said sarcastically, glaring at Parker. "Isabel was a nice girl, sweet and pretty. The sort of girl you think about getting serious with. And yeah, I guess some of it was my fault for taking her to that place. But she never would have fallen in with any of that if it wasn't for that goddamn leech. I don't care how bad he was hurt. Whether he actually did it himself or not, you can bet he's responsible."

"Lot of anger you've got toward folks you haven't seen lately," Freitas said.

Russell glared at her. "I got nothing against Isabel, not anymore," he said. "But that leech…it was him. They steal your soul, that's what the protesters say, and sometimes I think they're right. They steal your soul. They stole hers and they got her killed."

Russell strode past them to the door, and though he was trying to walk strong, Parker could see how rattled he was. He stopped and turned to Parker, ignoring Freitas. "My girlfriend's name is Rebecca Harris. She works on the fourth floor. She'll tell you I was with her."

He paused for a second. "I hope you catch the motherfuckers," he said. "Let 'em eat daylight."

Then he stalked out and slammed the door.

"Charming fellow," Parker said. "Isabel went out with that? Quiet, sweet Isabel?"

"I imagine he was a little more easygoing before his girl dumped him for a vampire," Freitas said. "And Isabel was…"

Freitas sat down, suddenly seeming tired. "That's when I met Isabel," she said. "I was investigating the murders at Nocturnal Urges, someone knocking off abusive patrons. Turned out the perp was Ryan's ex-wife Elyse Callahan and she was killed in the capture. But for a while, we thought Ryan did it."

"You arrested him, but let him go, right?" Parker said. "Isabel said—"

Freitas stared at the table. "I let him go after Isabel came to us and gave an alibi for Ryan," she said. "Even then, I was convinced he'd done it. Me, the guys on the squad, we all thought we had our guy. When Isabel came in, they tried to brush her off, send her away without reaching me because she'd fuck up an open-and-shut case with an alibi they were sure was fake."

Freitas kept talking as though Parker weren't even there. And for once, Parker tried to stay silent, not ask any questions that would make Freitas put up her walls again.

"She stood in the middle of the squad room and started shouting," Freitas said. "They all tried to shut her up, get her out before she fucked up the case. She just stood there screaming my name over and over until I heard her and came out to see what the fuck was going on. She was brave, you know, standing up to cops in our own station, but she had to do what was right because she knew Ryan was innocent. She just kept shouting my name. It was like I was the only one she trusted, the only one she thought could s-save..."

Freitas' voice trailed off.

Parker reached out a tentative hand to touch Freitas' shoulder. Instantly, Freitas snapped upright and her face was resolute again. "We'll check with Russell's girlfriend, but it doesn't matter," she said, her voice steely cold again.

"It doesn't?" Parker asked.

Freitas shook her head. "Can't you tell? He didn't do it either. Fuck."

* * * * *

Samantha didn't know what she expected to see. Perhaps the same Ryan she had seen in the hospital room, miserable and withdrawn. Certainly not the smiling, happy man she had danced with at the Christmas party to the laughter of their clapping friends. She was afraid that man was gone, as dead as Isabel, and might not ever return.

But the cold glitter in Ryan's eyes as he stood up from the wheelchair still took her by surprise. He was dressed in Danny's jeans and sweater, which hung a little loose on his spare frame. When she called Danny to ask him if he minded lending some clothes to Ryan, Danny had tried once again to talk her into letting him come with her. She declined, but seeing the look in Ryan's eyes, she wondered if it might not have been a mistake.

The only visible sign of injury was the thin line of stitches along the bloodless cut on the side of his head. Vampires didn't bruise when they were injured. Blood might seep out until healing took over, but the bleeding was nothing compared to what humans shed when they were hurt.

He stood at the counter and signed himself out. When he spoke, he didn't look at her.

"Did you arrange it?" he asked.

Samantha nodded. "Kelly Parker pulled a string or two."

"Good." Ryan finished signing and turned away from the desk clerk without a pause. "Let's go then."

Samantha led him through the hospital's dilapidated lobby, pausing only to wind a black scarf over her head to shield her face from the paltry winter sun. She offered Danny's baseball cap to Ryan, but he simply walked past her and out into the parking lot. He flinched a little as the sun struck his pale skin.

Samantha followed him to her car and unlocked the door for Ryan. His silence was something physical, an impenetrable wall, as she started the car and got moving.

Finally she couldn't be quiet any longer. "Ryan—"

"Don't," he said, his voice harsh. "Don't poke around in my head, Samantha."

"I'm not," she said. "I don't need a link to feel how much you're hurting. I can feel—"

"No, you can't," Ryan said roughly.

"Ryan, if not me, you should talk to someone," Samantha said.

Ryan laughed, a harsh, bitter sound without humor. "Are you suggesting I see a shrink, Samantha? How modern. I should lie down on a couch and share my feelings? Extra charge if the shrink can make me weep? That will bring Isabel back?"

"No," Samantha replied. "But I doubt she'd want you to tear yourself to pieces either."

"I have no intention of wallowing in angst," Ryan said. "I'm going to find whoever did this."

"And turn him over to Anne and Kelly, right? That's the plan?" Samantha asked sarcastically.

Ryan turned those glittering eyes toward her. "You know better than that," he said, deadly still. "If it's a human, they'll give him a nice chiding and put him in a prison where he can eat three meals a day and write a book about how humans and vampires shouldn't be allowed to be together, it's sinful and wrong and he's doing God's work."

"He's killed humans," Samantha pointed out.

"Humans shacked up with vampires are more worthless to them than the vampires themselves," Ryan spat. "You forget I have some familiarity with this, Samantha."

Samantha's brow furrowed. "I thought your first consort was a vampire?"

Ryan stared out the car window at the buildings they passed. "Elyse was human when I married her in Ireland," he said, his voice quieter. "We had to marry in secret, but she was my wife. Two men ran her down with a cart one day. For sport. I found her dying and turned her to save her life."

Samantha kept her hands on the wheel. "So that's why she…"

"Hated me and took out her fury on those men at the club," Ryan said, and a new tinge of sadness entered his voice.

Samantha had never heard him speak of Elyse, the coolly beautiful vampire who had worked with them at the club until the police discovered she was behind a string of dead Nocturnal Urges patrons. Samantha hadn't been there the day Elyse was killed during her arrest but she heard plenty about it.

"Ryan," she whispered. "Is it true? What they said? That you…"

"Killed her a second time," he said. "With the bite. She was wounded but she would have survived long enough for them to execute her. I gave her a merciful death. More merciful than my feeble attempt to save her."

"Ryan, what happened to Isabel was not your fault," Samantha said. "And for that matter, what happened to Elyse was not your fault either. The blame for Elyse lies with those men who ran her down, and as for the men she killed, the blame for that lies with Elyse herself. You cannot fault yourself for the actions of others. If I held myself responsible for everything Diego did…"

"I know," Ryan interrupted. "But the difference is the men in Ireland are long dead. Elyse is dead. Isabel is…dead. But the person who killed her is not. She deserves…"

"What, vengeance?" Samantha asked. "This isn't healthy, Ryan."

Ryan stared out the window. "Didn't your old master train you in the *Desafío*?"

Samantha rolled her eyes. "Cristoval was crazy for everything of the ancient ways," she said. "But there's two key points here—'ancient' and 'crazy'. Cristoval was mad as the proverbial hatter *and* a march hare by the time I broke with the kiss and ran, and no one outside Spain has practiced the *Desafío* ritual in nearly a century."

"I'm quite sure the scimitars in room four only need a little sharpening," Ryan said.

Samantha gritted her teeth and wished she'd let Danny come along. "Now you've really got me worried," she said. "Those are decorations! Ryan, I'm half tempted to turn this car around and take you back for another workup."

"Don't," he said, a pleading note to his voice.

Samantha kept driving. "All right, Ahab, what if the killer is a human? The *Desafío* is a vampire custom."

Ryan smiled humorlessly and she didn't like the chilly look in his eyes. "He won't get to write that book."

"They'd kill you," Samantha reminded him quietly.

"I don't care," he replied.

Samantha reached the morgue parking lot and pulled into the visitor spot. "Let's table this for now. Just promise me you'll keep your mouth shut about this vengeance stuff in front of the humans, okay? They will lock you up in an eastern-facing cell."

"I'm not stupid," Ryan said, getting out of the car. He still didn't look right to her, pale even for a vampire, and he wavered a bit on his feet.

Samantha moved beside him, not touching him, but standing close enough that he knew support was there if he needed it. "Ryan, have you fed today?"

"They gave me donated blood at the hospital," he said. "And there's cow's blood at the club."

Samantha led him toward the building. "Sooner or later you'll need a bite, Ryan."

"Donated blood," he said. "I don't intend to go back to the rooms, Samantha. I didn't give it up just for her."

Samantha flinched, remembering too clearly the years they both had spent servicing clients at the club. Neither of them had been on the list for full sexual services. But she had bitten more humans and ridden their pleasure more often than she could remember. She had left the club to work at the community center full-time and Ryan had been promoted to assistant manager. But the memories were strong, including the many times she and Ryan had playacted for the marks. It had never been sexual for them, any more than actors playing a scene in a movie automatically fall in love and bed each other. But they couldn't help but be friends, knowing each other as well as they did.

Joann Betschart was waiting for them inside, her face somber. "With all due respect, Mr. Callahan, you don't look well enough to be walking about," she said.

"I'm fine," Ryan said dully.

Betschart led them into a small, nondescript room with a curtained window on the far wall. "Are you sure about this?" she asked.

Ryan nodded.

Betschart pulled back the curtain. Samantha made a small sound in her throat. She couldn't help it.

Isabel's face was dreadfully pale with a bluish tint to her lips. They had thoughtfully covered her nude body with a sheet and turned her around so the gash in the side of her neck would not be visible. The wound that would never heal. The warmth and vibrant life that had danced before the fire was gone, sucked away in the cold, harsh glare of the fluorescent lights.

Samantha dropped her eyes and looked at Ryan.

Ryan stared at the window, his entire body stiff and immobile. That hard, glittering look in his eyes wavered and she saw the bottomless depths behind it. His fists clenched and unclenched, and she slid over beside him, touching his arm.

"I imagined...perhaps..." Ryan murmured in a small voice.

"It wasn't real," Samantha finished. "I'm so sorry, Ryan."

Betschart looked at them and when Samantha nodded, she closed the curtain. "I'm very sorry for your loss, Mr. Callahan," she said, and stepped out of the room.

Samantha turned back to Ryan. That cold glitter was back in his eyes and it made her take a step back.

"It's not just Isabel," he said. "Beth Sanford, Drew's consort. I saw the news."

Samantha silently cursed the Saint Abraham's nurses for not disconnecting his television.

* * * * *

Freitas was on her second drink when there was a knock at the door. She left the chain on as she opened the door until she saw Fradella's face. "Aw hell," she murmured.

"Thanks," he said sarcastically as she unlatched the chain. "You always know how to make me feel all warm and fuzzy, Anne."

"What do you want?" she sighed, turning away and walking back toward the small living room, still holding her drink.

Fradella followed her and immediately scooped up the service pistol laying on the table. He checked the clip. "Dammit, Anne," he said. "Fucking around with a loaded gun while you're on the sauce. I'm really impressed with your coping skills."

"Fuck you," Freitas said without heat, dropping back down on the couch. "I just forgot to unload it when I got home."

Fradella removed the clip and laid the gun back down on the table. "Great," he said. "I don't have to ask how you're doing, do I?"

"Spectacular," Freitas said, raising her glass. "Want a drink?"

"Not at the moment," he said, sitting down beside her. "Anne, she was a good friend. She deserved better than this. But this…reaction of yours, it's way out of line of anything I've ever seen from you. And I've known you a long damn time."

"Yeah," Freitas said, setting down the drink. "If you don't mind, I don't feel like sharing my feelings. 'Kay?"

"No," Fradella said, frowning at her. "It's not okay. Tell me what's bothering you, besides the obvious."

Freitas leaned back on the couch, her eyes closed. "Don't bug me, Frank," she said. "You always do this to me, you keep pushing, you want to know what's on my mind, you ask your questions over and over. Then you don't fuckin' like the answers and we end up yelling at each other until you storm out the door."

Fradella traced a gentle finger along her brow, below the brutally short haircut she had always kept. "Me walking out the door wasn't my idea," he reminded her gently.

"And what, you're waiting for it to open up again? Is that what this is about?" Freitas asked, still not opening her eyes.

Fradella sighed. "You just can't accept that I might be here because I'm worried as hell, can you? That maybe I have no ulterior motive except your safety and happiness?"

"I can take care of myself." Freitas started to get up and Fradella pulled her back down. For once, she let him.

"Anne." He spoke quietly. "Tell me. I know you were there when it went down. I can't imagine the frustration you must feel. But you could not possibly have known what was happening in that house."

Freitas would not look at him. "She trusted me," she said thickly. "She was just a kid, no older than Parker, and she trusted me to be...I don't know. Truth, justice and the American way, all that shit we used to believe in when we were young. Do you remember that, Frank? Remember when we were like Parker and Chapman and all those young kids out of the academy? When the bad guys got the handcuffs and we were on the side of the angels?"

"Vaguely," Fradella said, just to keep her talking.

Freitas had closed her eyes again. "That day she stood in the precinct, shouting down Ken Henry, shouting for me to come help her, chase away the shadows, let Ryan out with the power of the truth or some such idealistic nonsense. That's when she became a friend, but also, I don't know…"

"A daughter?" Fradella asked.

Freitas opened her eyes and stared at him. "That's so movie of the week I may have to smack you," she said. "I'm nowhere near old enough to be Isabel's mother."

"Or Parker's for that matter, but you have kind of taken them both in that way," Fradella pointed out.

"Oh whatever," Freitas said without heat. "Isabel's dead and we're fuckin' nowhere on it, Frank. We got nothing. Now Sanford's wife is toast and God knows how many more this fuck'll get before we stop him. If we can stop him. As Diego proved, we are not exactly well equipped for a vampire psycho or three, and yet we seem to be getting more than our fair share of them."

"Let Chris Cox worry about that," Fradella said.

Freitas snorted. "Parker's right about Cox, you know," she said quietly. "She's young and impulsive but her contacts are good. She's hearing shit you and I will never hear, and she hears he's wrong, Frank. Wrong to the bone, worse since Diego went batshit on those four boys from his team."

"We can't do anything about Cox and right now there's nothing we can do about the firebug," Fradella pointed out. "You're carrying too much, Anne. You should take a few days and rest, let it go. You can't do all the policing in this city by yourself. Not even you."

Freitas reached out and held Fradella's hand gently in hers. "He asked her to marry him, Frank. At the party."

Fradella closed his eyes. "Damn. That's the missing ring in Joann's report?"

"The betrothal ring or whatever you call it for vamp-human partners when they can't marry," Freitas said. "Knelt down right in front of the fireplace. Just like you."

Fradella drew her close and for once she let him. He wrapped his arms around her shoulders and she rested her head on his chest, still impossibly small for a woman with so much power and force to her. She was still coiled tight, still not letting go. But she let him hold her and it seemed to him a bit of the tension eased from her to him. It had always been like this, always been Anne behind her walls, not letting him near her even when they were as intimate as a man and a woman can be. But he had long ago accepted that this was where Anne needed him — arm's length, no closer.

And she never, ever, cried in front of him.

* * * * *

Parker was getting heartily sick of the hospital. She had finally convinced Freitas to go home and rest, though the glint in her partner's eyes remained as steely as ever. She doubted Freitas would actually sleep.

Parker walked into the lobby of Saint Abraham's and immediately tripped over some loose tiles on the floor. She bumped into a hulking form. "Damn, Flanigan, how tall are you?" she asked, sighing.

"Taller than my father, which annoyed him no end," Flanigan replied. "And do I dare ask what brings you to Saint Abraham's?"

"Same thing as you, I bet," Parker said. "Cox is gone, time to have a chat with Mr. Sanford."

"You know, you're a breath away from interfering with a multiple-homicide investigation," Flanigan said, but his voice was easy.

"Hey, we're letting you guys talk to them first," Parker returned.

Flanigan pointed to the desk. "Looks like we're almost too late."

Drew Sanford stood at the desk, signing himself out. He was dressed in a plain—but immaculate and clearly just-purchased—T-shirt and jeans, which rather surprised Parker. Every time she had seen the respected vampire, in person or in real life, he had been in a suit or other more formal attire.

"Mr. Sanford," Flanigan said, pulling out his investigation as he walked toward the desk. "I'm Jon Flanigan with the state fire marshal's arson investigation team. Can I talk to you for just a minute?"

Sanford didn't look up as he signed his name on the third of seven papers. The attendant looked bored as she connected incoming calls, ignoring them. "I have already spoken with Lieutenant Cox. Surely you can glean whatever information you need from him."

"Lieutenant Cox has different questions," Flanigan said. "My specialty is arson, theirs is murder."

"In this case, they are one and the same," Sanford replied, his voice even. "While I appreciate what you and the detective did for me, I must now go about the business of burying my consort. I would appreciate some measure of privacy."

"Mr. Sanford, we don't want to invade your privacy," Parker interjected. "But we do want to find whoever did this. You want us to find him, don't you?"

Sanford turned to her, a cool mask instead of his face. "I'm sure you will apply all your considerable talents to the case," he said. "You are welcome to inspect the remnants of my home and to read the reports of Lieutenant Cox and his fine squad. But for now, I must ask you to leave me alone."

Flanigan seemed to accept defeat. "Very well, sir," he said, pressing a business card into Sanford's hand. "If you think of anything else you'd like to tell us, please give me a call."

Sanford nodded and turned to leave, putting on an overcoat. Parker called after him, "Where can we find you?"

Sanford turned back to her, his eyes hollow and blank in that unfathomable mask. "Why would you need to find me?"

Parker blinked. "If we find the guy. *When* we find the guy. To let you know."

Sanford seemed frozen, as if it hadn't even occurred to him. "Call my office," he said, and turned back to leave, settling an old-fashioned fedora—incongruous with his T-shirt and windbreaker—on his head before stepping out into the fading sunlight.

Parker frowned. "Doesn't think we'll catch the guy. Doesn't even consider it a possibility. That's odd."

"Odd my ass," Flanigan said. "I'm no cop but I can tell when someone's hiding something."

Parker grinned. "You talk like a cop."

Flanigan shook his head. "Firefighter, switched to arson investigation six years ago," he said. "I've seen plenty of firebugs, torching for fun and profit. Sanford there, he's no bug, but he knows who did it."

"Well, he knows something," Parker said, following Flanigan out into the parking lot. The sun was setting, coloring the sky a pale orange, quickly moving toward darkness. Flanigan's car was parked not far from hers, the only two with a detachable emergency bubble on the top.

"I bet he didn't give it to Cox," Flanigan mused.

Parker gritted her teeth. "That son of a bitch hates vamps, hates anyone who associates with vamps and is about as pleasant as a cockroach with a hangover," she said. "Whatever Sanford had, he didn't spill it to Cox."

"I kind of got the feeling Cox wasn't giving this case his full attention," Flanigan said ruefully. He opened his car door. "You'll let me know if something comes to mind, right?"

"First call. Well, second, after my partner," Parker amended. "No offense."

"Of course," Flanigan said, and waved farewell before getting into his car.

Parker watched him drive off then went around to her own car. Lost in thought, she got in, waving the air a little at the faint smell of Freitas' cigarette smoke.

"Detective," whispered a voice from the backseat.

"Shit!" Parker shouted, her hand instantly dropping down to her service pistol. A steel grip grasped her around the neck and pulled her back against the seat.

"Drop the gun, my dear, or you'll never eat solid food again," the voice whispered, pressing a thumb against the hard bones in the back of her neck. It was a smooth, male voice, promising sickly sweet treats and decadence in its sultry hiss.

Parker let her hand fall away from the gun and raised her hands to the wheel, her heart pounding in fear. *Diego, motherfuck it's Diego, he's back and Samantha didn't sense it, fuck I'm fucked it's fucking DIEGO...*

"Relax, my dear, I wish you no harm," the voice whispered, a sibilant hiss in her ear. "Your delightful Lieutenant Cox and the bumbling fireboy are of no concern. You, however, are beginning to vex me. Wherever I go, there you are. You and your lovely partner."

Language is too formal for Diego, even with pretensions, thought the part of Parker that remembered she was a cop. She tried to calm down, think it through. No one was visible in the cold gray twilight of the hospital parking lot.

"What do you want?" Parker asked.

"Shhh," the voice whispered. "Meddle not in the affairs of vampires, for we shall inherit the earth. What shall become of our food when we walk our streets again?"

Not Diego but just as fuckin' crazy. Parker tried to figure how she could break the grip before the nut bar in the back managed to break her neck. She glanced up at the rearview mirror but it showed nothing. He was definitely a vampire.

In the darkening light, Parker saw Flanigan's car circling back into the parking lot. Her sudden flash of relief was immediately extinguished by added pressure on her neck. Her hand slid slowly down the side of the steering wheel.

"If you touch the horn, your friend will die as well and I will finish your lovely partner at my leisure," the voice hissed.

Frustration and anger welled up inside Parker. She wanted to turn, to strike at him, to fight him, as she knew she could. She was no vampire but she could give him a memorable fight at least. But the image of being trapped in a hospital bed, unable to move, unable to breathe or eat on her own, a living death trapped inside her wasting body... *He picked the right threat. Smart fucker.*

"How do I know it's really you who did it?" Parker asked.

"I have the lovely girl's ring," the voice whispered. "I do not need this."

A perfectly smooth, marble-white hand — definitely a man's hand, by the bone structure — reached over Parker's left shoulder and dropped something in her lap — a small book, bound in brown leather with gold-leaf edges. A diary.

Then the hand slid against her cheek, cool to the touch with long, talon-like fingernails that scratched lightly along her jaw before tracing the bite scar on the side of her neck. Parker shuddered, unable to move, hating herself for being afraid. A tiny tear escaped the corner of her eye and she hated it as well.

"Do not move," he said, and suddenly the hands were gone from her neck. The door opened and instantly Parker had her gun out and leaped from the car. She leveled the gun in all directions, bracing herself against the side of the car, her heart pounding even harder.

Flanigan pulled up beside her and jumped out of his car, engine still running. "Parker! What is it?"

"Shut up!" Parker shouted, scanning the lot. She moved between the cars, her heart pounding, the gun pointed every way she could see.

No one was there.

"Goddammit!" she shouted, moving back toward her car. "Goddamn motherfucker, goddammit!"

Parker holstered the gun, leaning against her car next to the still-open door. "Fuck," she whispered, and another tear escaped.

"Hey," Flanigan said. "What the hell is—"

"He was here," Parker said. "He was fucking here and I–" She shuddered, fighting it. She struck the side of her car with a balled-up fist and succeeded only in slightly denting the metal.

"Hey," Flanigan said, and laid a clumsy hand on her shoulder. She looked up at him for a moment and almost thought she could literally cry on his shoulder. There was concern in his face, kind and worried.

Then Parker got hold of herself. She looked into the car and there on the floor of the driver's seat was the diary. "We have a clue," she said.

* * * * *

Nocturnal Urges was just barely starting its night with a handful of patrons when Samantha and Ryan arrived. The Creatures of the Night were setting up their equipment on the stage. Ryan stumbled a little and Brent, the hulking bouncer who stood at the door of the club every night, helped steady him alongside Samantha.

Fiona swept across the floor, ready for the evening in one of her trademark ball gowns, a deep green silk that offset her flaming red hair. "Ryan dear, you look dreadful," she said. "Brent, go fetch him some blood. Human stock, third shelf on the fridge." Brent silently vanished, obedient as always.

Ryan shook his head. "I'm not hungry, Fiona."

"Nonsense," Fiona said briskly. "You look like a stiff wind would knock you over. Samantha, help me get him into a room."

"No," Ryan protested.

Samantha rolled her eyes. "No clients," she said. "Right, Fiona?"

"Of course not," Fiona said. "You're in no shape to entertain. But we will take care of you."

Samantha and Fiona walked with Ryan across the club's darkened interior, past a few curious patrons, toward the dark recesses of the rooms where vampires serviced human patrons. Andi and David, two vampire friends of Samantha's, stood by the bar with sorrow in their eyes. Everyone had heard, Samantha realized, and no one knew what to say.

Room four was like the others—gothic, with a four-poster bed and candelabras for lighting. Ryan lay down on the bed, still seeming weak.

Brent arrived with a container of warmed blood. Ryan still turned away but Samantha nudged him. "Drink it or I swear I'll make you."

"You and what army?" Ryan muttered.

Samantha smiled gently. "Right now I could do it by myself. But I'd let Brent help just so you wouldn't feel your manliness slighted," she said.

Brent folded his arms in his best immovable-bouncer pose.

Ryan sighed, sat up and drank. Almost immediately his color improved, though he still didn't seem like himself.

"There, that's better," Fiona said. "How long can you stay with him, Samantha?"

Samantha glanced at her watch. "I'm supposed to meet Danny and his father at the community center at seven but it's only a few blocks from here," she said.

"Humph," Fiona muttered, and Samantha smiled. She and Fiona had known each other almost all Samantha's long life, dating back to their mutual binding in Cristoval's kiss. Fiona had never approved of Samantha's decision to leave the anonymity of the club and blamed Danny for it. "Well, I'll send Andi back to help shortly. She's got a light docket tonight."

"Tell her to behave," Samantha said, smiling a little.

Fiona and Brent left them alone and Samantha found a velvet wrap to place over Ryan as an extra blanket. He sipped a bit more blood, grimacing.

"The club soda prevents clotting," Samantha said.

"Tastes like nothing. Must be the smoke. Everything's tasteless now," Ryan said dully.

Samantha touched his hand gently. "I wish I could stay. I'll check back with you later tonight."

"Nonsense," Ryan said. "You go spend some time with your young man. It's Christmas after all."

Samantha grinned. "My young man. You act like I'm robbing the cradle."

"Well, you're about ninety years older than he is, right?" Ryan said, with the barest ghost of his old smile.

"Eighty-two, I'll have you know," she said imperiously. "Besides, he has an old soul."

"Sure," he said, and sipped more blood. "You know how lucky you are, right? How rare and beautiful it is?"

Samantha softened, smiling. "Yes. I know."

"And you know it doesn't last."

Her smile faded. "I know," she said quietly. "But I'm looking forward to another seventy-odd years with Danny before I lose him."

Abaddon

Ryan gazed down at the blood, his face harsh and miserable. "The protesters are right, we should never be allowed to marry humans," he said, his voice breaking. "We have no business loving them."

Samantha gripped his hand more tightly. "Ryan, you're speaking from pain right now. I know you don't regret loving Isabel."

"No," he said without hesitation. "I wasn't alive before Isabel. Not even with Elyse. Never before...and never again. But she—"

"She was loved," Samantha said forcefully. "To be loved, truly loved for all that she is and all that she can be, just once in her life. That is the greatest gift anyone can give another person, human or vampire, and you gave that to her, so don't you ever regret a moment of it on her behalf. She wouldn't want that."

Ryan turned his face away and she let him, knowing he could not face her with the pain so fresh in his eyes. He stared at the far wall and she followed his gaze to the three scimitars arrayed on the wall. They rested in a curious three-pronged design with one slanted diagonally and the other two diverging from it. They were actually shamshirs, Persian swords with a pronounced curve to the tip but in modern times, everyone called them scimitars. The handles were engraved with a pattern resembling flames, a tiny skull etched on the end of the handle and an intricate pattern etched along the long, curved blades.

"Ryan, stop it," Samantha said, trying to interject a little strength into her voice. "Those swords are decorative."

"They're from the Middle East, from Cristoval's armory," Ryan said.

Samantha gaped. "How did you know that?"

"Fiona brought them here when the kiss..." Ryan stopped.

"When the humans killed Cristoval and the rest of the kiss, except for Diego," Samantha finished. "I wasn't there, Ryan, you don't have to tiptoe around it. I broke with the kiss long before then."

Ryan looked over at her. "How did you do that? I always meant to ask you. I thought once you were bound into a kiss, you could not break out without the permission of the master vampire."

Samantha glanced away, suddenly uncomfortable. "It's hard to say," she said. "My mental powers grew the longer I was with them and after Todd… I found I had the strength to ease farther and farther from Cristoval's grip. It took a few practice tries, seeing how far I could get, but one night I threw everything I had into breaking the link and running away before he could catch me."

This time it was Ryan who held her hand with something akin to his old strength—the blood was really working, she thought. "You were very brave."

Samantha cleared her throat. "Bravery would have been challenging Cristoval for the kiss. Destroying him would have freed them all. Instead, they died with the mob coming for Diego because Cristoval would not stop his madness."

"Is it my turn for 'you can't blame yourself'?" Ryan said, and Samantha smiled.

Then it hit her, a sudden pain at the back of her head as though someone had struck her hard with a two-by-four. She cried out involuntarily, reaching behind her head, half expecting to feel blood on her fingers.

"What's wrong?" Ryan asked, staring at her.

"Oh God!" she cried again, smelling smoke as the ache settled deeper into the back of her head.

"Samantha!"

"Oh no, Danny," Samantha whispered. "Danny!"

Ryan suddenly understood and threw the blankets aside. "Oh shit," he whispered, reaching out to her hand.

Samantha threw off his grasp and ran out of the room, barreling past a very surprised Andi, who stumbled back as Ryan followed her out into the club.

Samantha kept running, through the club and past Brent at the door to the darkened street outside. In her panic, she forgot about her car, running north toward the community center. She could already see smoke rising into the night sky above the streetlights. She ran, her legs moving faster and faster, driven by sheer terror.

A siren sounded somewhere and Samantha kept running, and now she remembered her car, and it might have been faster to take the car but it was only another two blocks now. Somewhere behind her Ryan was pursuing her but could not hope to keep up in his current state. She needed no air, running with silent, frantic speed toward the pillar of smoke she could see clearly now. Her heart could not beat, but it felt as though it pounded through her body, the fear coupled with the silence in her mind, a terrible silence, ominous and deep.

The community center was engulfed in orange flames, rising out of the roof with large glowing bits of debris vanishing into the cold night sky. Two trucks were already deployed with firefighters training their hoses on the blaze. Another truck pulled up, flashing lights and screaming sirens, just as Samantha came into sight.

"Danny!" she screamed, the pain in her head growing worse with every second and her pace did not slow as she reached the sidewalk in front of the center. A firefighter grabbed her and she hit him hard, knocking him down as she struggled toward the burning building. The heat was intense and she could hear the other firefighters shouting at her to get back…

Then someone's arms wrapped around her waist, hauling her back from the flames. Someone strong. A vampire. Ryan.

"Danny! Danny's in there! Danny!" she shouted, struggling against him. Weakened as he was, Ryan held her tight, and over his shoulder she could see Brent loping after them.

"They'll help him, they'll find him!" Ryan cried, but Samantha knew he was just mouthing words.

"Danny!" she screamed again, struggling. "Let me go, goddammit!"

Ryan's feet slipped in the water cascading down from the house and they both fell to the sidewalk in front of the community center. Samantha reached out with her mind, trying to find Danny, to feel him at the other end of the link.

There was nothing but the silent white void and the intense pain in her head.

Samantha screamed again, her still heart shattering in the horrible sound of her own voice. Ryan held her tightly, his shoulders shaking, and for the first time she could sense his thoughts, his sorrow and misery compounding with hers.

"Oh God, Samantha, I'm so sorry," Ryan murmured.

"No," she whispered, and finally stopped fighting him. The tears welled up without release, the sorrow too huge for her to contain in her chest. "He's not…"

Ryan clutched her shoulders more tightly and she could hear him repeating it to himself with Freitas and Parker standing over him in the hospital room, *It's not true, not gone, it can't be.*

Samantha cried out again, a sound that came from somewhere deep in her heart, misery and unspeakable loss, and somewhere in Ryan's mind, she saw the trio of scimitars, an image burned bright in his mind and imprinted on hers, a sign of vengeance.

More sirens, more flashing lights, and she knelt in the water and the mud with Ryan's arms still wrapped around her. She could not speak. Brent stood over them, silent and immobile. Past him, she saw a car pull up and Robert Carton leapt out of it without turning off the engine. He ran toward the fire and the same firefighter who Samantha had decked stopped him.

"Is my son in there? Is Danny–" Robert stopped, seeing Samantha still being restrained by Ryan. "Danny?"

Samantha raised her eyes to Robert's and watched his face twist in sudden horror and shock. "Oh Christ," Robert whispered. "Christ, no."

A crowd had started to form, young people from the neighborhood and vampires from the club. Andi and David stood by Red, the gang leader who had kept the peace in the neighborhood for the past several years. Some of the younger ones were crying on each others' shoulders. Samantha saw Celia, hovering in the background like a ghost, watching the flames with the others.

Lucas stood beside Celia, the smoke swirling past the kids and making them cough as he argued with the scene commander. "He was in the living room, he wasn't far from the door, you've got to..." Lucas trailed off when he saw Samantha staring at him, his face miserable.

A car with a flashing bubble light pulled up behind Robert's sedan and Parker and Flanigan leaped out. Flanigan ran up to the scene commander, flashing his badge and firing questions. Parker moved over beside Robert, who was ranting something Samantha couldn't quite hear and didn't care to. It didn't seem as if she would care about anything again. The ache in her head had settled into a dull pain and the smell of the smoke was real now.

Her fists clenched against Ryan's chest, and she heard him murmur, "I know. I know."

"*Desafío*," she whispered. "It's not enough."

"It's never enough," he whispered back.

Chapter Four

ೞ

December 2

Christopher stopped by the office again with yet another donation. He has been so generous with us and has asked for nothing. Until tonight, at least — it was late and I was the only one left in the office. He asked me if I cared to join him for dinner.

What could I say? It would have been so rude to decline when I obviously had no plans and he has been so generous with us. Of course I told him I would call Drew and ask him to join us. I knew Drew would not answer his phone — he has a city council meeting tonight and he will be there until all hours, simply sitting in the audience as a physical reminder to the councilmen that vampires exist. But it seemed only proper to call, if only to remind Christopher that I am, if not a married woman, a committed one.

I surprised myself by having a wonderful time! Christopher took me to this lovely little place downtown, and after a delightful meal we walked up and down Beale Street and marveled at how far the city has come in such a short time. It seems only a few years ago that one could not walk down Beale without fearing for one's life. Now it is so vibrant and cheerful, and there is nothing to fear. Even if there were, I felt perfectly safe with him. He is European of course, but he exudes this sense of danger. It's strange.

And we laughed! I didn't realize until he drove me back to my car at the office that it has been literally months since I laughed with Drew. And that took away all the humor as I puzzled it out.

For a long time now Drew and I have been like roommate and partner, not husband and wife. He is as thoughtful as ever, considers my opinion and tells me about...work. We talk about work. And occasionally the house.

Sometimes I look in the mirror and I see an old woman looking out at me. I know I'm not really old yet — forty-eight is hardly decrepit. But Drew looks as young as he did three hundred years ago. How can he still find me attractive, exciting, as I age before his eyes?

Perhaps he doesn't. Perhaps that's why we haven't laughed together in so long. Perhaps that's why my dinner with Christopher — perfectly innocuous, mind you — seems now like a shining bright spot in what has become a dull and dreary routine.

I know perfectly well how dangerous these thoughts are. And Christopher — he's hardly my age either, perhaps mid-thirties. But I lay awake last night until Drew came home, and when he came to bed, I told him I had had dinner with a donor. And he was not at all interested.

Is his mind already moving forward? He has had eight consorts before me. Am I just another in a long line of companions? Is he already thinking of the one who will follow me?

Sometimes I wonder if he knows I'm still here. And that I still love him.

* * * * *

Celia's fists slammed over and over into the practice dummy. Her knuckles were wrapped in protective bandages as she alternated between a hook and a cross, pounding away at the dummy until it fell over.

Sensei shook his head. "Still too much emotion," he said. Sensei was a man of small frame, an unassuming human with graying blond hair. He gave no hint of his immense skill and lightning reflexes, which often made people take him for granted.

"Well, it's an emotional time," Parker said from the entrance, slipping off her shoes. She bowed respectfully to Sensei, a reflex borne of her years of training in the dojo even before she became a police officer.

"What the fuck are you doing here?" Celia snapped, hauling the dummy back up.

Sensei's hand snapped out and caught Celia's arm. "There will be no disrespect," he warned.

Immediately Celia backed down. "Sorry, Sensei."

Parker came over to her. "Haven't seen you in the last few days," she said. "I wanted to see if you're okay."

"Fine," Celia said, stretching out her arms. "Just working out. No school to miss so you don't gotta harp at me."

Parker folded her arms. "I do have to know where you are," she said. "You know what would happen if your caseworker just happened to drop by for a visit and I have to admit that I have no idea where you've been for two days?"

Celia shrugged. "Don't give a—"

Sensei cleared his throat.

"Don't care about the stupid caseworker, she's a…dimwit," Celia amended.

That was hard to argue. The caseworker was a cheerfully naïve woman who wore teddy bear T-shirts and brought books for Celia that were about six years too young for her.

"She has the power to pull you out of my care and put you in a home," Parker said. "Does that get your attention?"

"Should it?" Celia jabbed a few light punches at the dummy.

Parker glanced down, stung. "I saw you at the fire scene," she said more softly. "You doing okay?"

"I didn't get burned," Celia said. "Me 'n Lucas, we was elsewhere, ya know what I mean."

Parker gritted her teeth. "That's not what I meant. You know about—"

"Doesn't take a genius, Danny's car was parked right in front and Lucas saw him inside right before the place went up," Celia returned. "And Samantha's freak-out was kind of a hint."

Sensei stepped between Celia and the dummy. "You betray your weakness," he said calmly.

"Ain't got no fuckin' weakness," Celia snapped back, forgetting to watch her language. "What, you expect me to fall down and cry like a kid?"

"Danny and Samantha were kind to you, as much a part of your new family as Kelly here," Sensei said. "To pretend these losses mean nothing to you is cowardice."

"Fuck you!" Celia shouted, and started to push Sensei away. Parker involuntarily moved to smack her or hug her, she wasn't sure which.

But Sensei was faster—he was always faster—and held Celia's arms still.

"To face loss and let yourself feel takes true bravery," Sensei said, his eyes boring into Celia's with intensity. "You have not wept for Isabel or Danny, or reached out to Ryan and Samantha. You push away even Kelly, who has shared her home with you and done so much for you. This does not make you strong. It is weakness."

He released her arms then, still staring into her angry gray eyes.

Celia dropped her gaze first. "I saw Ryan with Samantha," she said in a more hesitant voice. "They let him out of the hospital?"

"Yeah," Parker said, feeling as if she were literally walking on eggshells—already half-cracked. But then she often felt that way around Celia, as though any wrong step would crash her through the floor into dangerous territory. "It's been rough on him. Tell you the truth, we're all a little... I mean, at first we didn't know if you were in Ryan and Isabel's house, since you just vanished from the party."

"Was gone before it went up," Celia said, stretching out her legs and twisting her torso so she wouldn't be looking at either of them. "Didn't see nothing."

Parker wanted to reach out and touch her shoulder, but she knew from experience that Celia wouldn't react well to that. She didn't like to be touched. "Will you come home tonight?"

Celia shrugged. "Probably." She returned to the dummy, kicking it in the head over and over.

Parker bowed again to Sensei, who walked with her toward the door of the dojo as she slipped her shoes back on. Once outside in the chilled December air, she was able to exhale. "That girl has more armor than the Chain Gang," she mused ruefully.

"Funny you should mention them," Sensei said.

Parker sighed. "How bad is it?"

Sensei gazed out at the street where only a few cars passed in the darkness. "It's getting to be quite unhealthy to be a vampire on the street these days," he said. "I know of at least one vampire who was badly beaten this week. He knows they were on the Chain Gang and off-duty."

"Will he testify?" Parker asked helplessly.

Sensei didn't bother to dignify her question with an answer. "There is much anger growing among the vampires, Kelly," he said. "They are tired of being treated as second-class citizens—third-class, now that Tunstall's Law has passed. More and more of them are restless and their anger is just as strong at the humans who reach out to them as those who despise them. Soon there will be a schism that will take great lengths to cross."

"Christ, Sensei, there has to be a way to stop it," Parker said. "Other than me simply bashing Chris Cox over the head and muzzling that idiot Renfrow."

Sensei gazed out at the street again. "I hear of a unifying force among the vampires," he said slowly. "There is more cohesion among them than once there was. They are beginning to speak with a single voice. But I am concerned about this voice. It does not speak of equality with the humans. It speaks of dominating them."

Parker stared up at the sky, wishing she could just wave a wand and make everyone sit down and behave. "Sometimes I don't get you, Sensei," she said. "You talk about humans and vampires as though you're neither."

Sensei gave a small, wry smile. "Someone has to be Switzerland," he said.

* * * * *

Freitas and Samantha rode in silence. No music played and no words of comfort were exchanged. Samantha stared out the window, trying to think of anything other than the ache in her heart or the trial that lay before her. But it was as though a hole had been drilled through her heart and she could not help returning to it, as a person whose tooth has been pulled cannot help exploring the empty hole it leaves.

Freitas pulled out a cigarette without asking if it bothered her. She lit it with the dashboard lighter and the smoke filled the car. In truth, Samantha had often smoked—as a vampire, she had no fear of cancer or other disease. She had refrained for months for Danny's sake. Now she reached out in silent plea and Freitas handed her a cigarette without speaking. Samantha inhaled the smoke, but it brought nothing, no solace.

Ryan was in the backseat. He had finally fallen asleep, though he must have dreamed—his face twitched in his slumber. They had left with Freitas when she came to the fire scene, not long after the roof fell in. They did not wait for the police and firefighters to begin the post-mortem on the still-burning remains of the community center. Freitas had barely started to ask before Samantha agreed and Ryan insisted on joining them.

Freitas turned the car onto the off-ramp and followed the state highway away from the interstate. The change in motion woke Ryan, who coughed a little at the smoke in the car. Samantha rolled down the window for a moment, letting the smoke out, before the chill of the December air made her roll it back up. She and Freitas both stubbed out their cigarettes.

The smell of the smoke was suddenly nauseating, choking Samantha, reminding her of the flames consuming the community center, consuming Danny...

"Pull over," Samantha said suddenly, and Freitas rolled onto the shoulder without a question. Samantha shoved the door open and stumbled away from the car, retching. She vomited blood, hideously red and sinking in steam on the white snow.

Danny's blood, she thought, remembering feeding gently from him, feeling his ecstasy at the feeding, holding him so close to her, knowing how fragile his life was but somehow so sure he would always be with her. Forever.

The last time, she thought, and it made her retch again, vomiting more blood, the pounding in her head unrelenting. It wasn't all Danny's blood, she had drunk a little stored blood since the last time she had been with him. But somehow the thought that she would never again feed from him, share that most intimate kiss with him, as intimate as the joining of their bodies in passion, made her whole body and soul twist in pain. Unbidden, tears came to her eyes, tears she tried to swallow as Ryan knelt beside her, his hand on her shoulder.

He would not tell her it was all right to cry, she knew. Once she started crying, she would never stop. What they were about to face needed strength and calm. The black despair roiled inside her, rising up to overwhelm her, but she held it off. Not yet.

Samantha reached out and gripped Ryan's hand, wiping her mouth with the back of a shaking hand. His hand held hers tightly and his strength helped her stand again. Freitas remained sitting behind the wheel, silent. She had opened her own window to let the smoke out of the car.

They got back in and kept rolling. Samantha's hands were shaking from more than the cold. When the car pulled through the gate, past the sentries to the parking lot of the Wallsh Institute, she felt a shiver run along her arms that had nothing to do with the cold.

Freitas showed her ID at the door and the security staff led the three of them through endless hallways of overbright fluorescent-lit cinderblock. Samantha was trying to keep calm, to hold tight to herself and not sense any more than she had to. They were frisked and sent through a metal detector, then frisked again. Samantha moved mechanically, doing as she was told without speaking.

"You can do this," Ryan said softly.

At the third checkpoint, a dark-haired man in a button-down shirt with glasses was waiting for them. "Detective, I'm Dr. Michael Hickerson," he said, shaking hands with Freitas. "We spoke on the phone."

"I assume everything's all right? We'll get to talk with him?" Freitas asked.

Dr. Hickerson led them into another room, a place that seemed comfortable and normal if one failed to notice how the table and chairs were rounded and nothing sharp was in sight. "You'll get to talk to him," he said. "He has displayed no further indications toward violence. But I am concerned that Ms. Crews intends to be present. As I told you on the phone…"

"Samantha is vital," Freitas said. "No one understands him like she does."

Dr. Hickerson glanced over at Samantha, who remained silent. "Well, that may be so," he said slowly. "But understand our purpose here is to try to bring back the man inside him—"

"That's fine. Have a ball mucking around in his head when we're gone," Freitas snapped. "Our purpose is to catch a killer. You know I can get a court order. Only it might mean a few more dead bodies before a judge gets around to signing it."

Dr. Hickerson held up a hand. "I'm not trying to be difficult," he said. "But I would like to be present at the interrogation."

"More the merrier," Freitas said.

Dr. Hickerson looked over at Ryan. "I'm sorry, you are—"

"Ryan Callahan, moral support," Freitas interjected. "He stays."

The guard tapped on the door and Dr. Hickerson opened it. A short, middle-aged man shuffled in, his hands bound in soft restraints. He looked up at Samantha and she was startled by his face. The last time she had seen Jeff Morris, he had been hale and strong, somewhat overweight, with a full beard and blustering manner. The man in front of her was at least thirty pounds thinner. The beard was gone and there was much more gray in his hair. There were wrinkles around his eyes and his florid face was paler now.

Dr. Hickerson pointing to Samantha. "Jeff, do you remember her?"

Samantha sat down at the table across from Morris with Freitas and Ryan standing behind her.

"Samantha," Morris said.

Samantha could sense Morris' uncertainty and fear. He was remembering that night at the park, remembering lifting the gun with a hand controlled by something beyond him. Unconsciously, his hand rose a bit, as if still holding the gun.

Morris and Samantha flinched in unison, each remembered the moment he fired the gun at Danny and Celia, and struck Samantha instead. Unconsciously she rubbed the spot at the center of her breastbone, the thin scar where the bullet had penetrated, and her headache thickened into something living and beating behind her eyes.

"It's all right, Mr. Morris," Samantha said. "It wasn't your fault."

Morris stared at her, his eyes confused and dulled by drugs. "I'm glad you're okay," he said in a small, childlike voice. Despite herself, Samantha felt sorry for him. He had been a blustering man more concerned with getting Robert Carton elected than any overriding sense of public service. She still believed he knew what he was doing when he strangled Meredith Schwartz to keep her from revealing Robert's secret trips to Nocturnal Urges. But he hadn't deserved what happened to him.

"Mr. Morris," Samantha said. "I need to talk to Diego."

Morris flinched at the name as if she had struck him. "I don't want to," he said in that plaintive voice.

Samantha's eyes filled with sorrow. "I know," she said. "I'm sorry, it's important."

Morris looked down, shaking his head back and forth and muttering, "No, no," over and over.

"It's okay, Jeff," Dr. Hickerson said. "You do whatever feels right to you."

"Doctor," Freitas warned.

Dr. Hickerson glared at her. "I realize a lot of law enforcement doesn't recognize Renfield Syndrome, but at least you could respect—"

"I recognize Renfield Syndrome, Doctor," Freitas snapped. "I saw this particular case up close and personal."

"Mr. Morris?" Samantha said. "Jeff? Can you at least tell me if Diego is here?"

Morris' voice came from his hunched-over body, small and frightened. "He's here."

"Shit," Freitas whispered.

"Here in Memphis?" Samantha asked.

Morris shook his head hard. "Here...with me."

Samantha leaned forward. "Jeff, is Diego the one doing the fires?"

"Fires…" Morris whispered. "Lovely dancing fires, they eat and eat and eat…"

"I knew it," Freitas growled.

Morris's head snapped up in a sudden movement that made everyone jump back, startled. The frightened, drugged patient was gone. His face split into a macabre grin, blackly jovial. His eyes glinted with mad humor.

"Miran-da," he singsonged.

Samantha stumbled back out of her chair, fighting the urge to run from the room. Only Ryan's steadying arm touching her shoulder kept her still.

"That's not my name," she said.

Morris tilted his head sideways, still grinning. "Oh Miranda, such misery," he gloated. "It's deeeeelicious."

Samantha tried to fend him off but she could feel Diego's power sinking into her. He had nearly enveloped her in his kiss before his capture and eventual escape from the police. The connection was there and it was all she could do to keep him out of her thoughts. Her headache pulsed with the onslaught. *He's so much more powerful,* she thought in panic.

"Diego," Samantha said. "Did you do this?"

"So sorry about your boy," Morris said, still grinning with hideous good cheer. "Such pain…it's exquisite. Much clearer than the first time, bitter and hot. Like fresh blood. Scrumptious."

Samantha shuddered and despite herself, her memory drew up the image he wanted her to see, to relive.

"Samantha, what's he talking about?" Freitas asked.

"Todd," Samantha said softly. "He was a cop in Chicago, in 1976. I was going to run away with him. Cristoval caught us."

"Sooo tasty," Morris chanted, licking his fingers. "Right in front of you, dear Miranda. I wanted to taste you too but Cristoval wouldn't let me. He always spoiled the best fun."

Samantha closed her eyes, willing her mind to stay in control, to fend off the image of Todd's torn-apart body. It was hard, so many things Diego was trying to see, and even reaching her through Morris, she was having trouble defending herself against the mental onslaught. She was suddenly afraid that if she were in the room with Diego himself instead of a human under his control, she would lose the battle for her own soul.

"Oh Miranda," Morris said. "You kept that poor boy-cop's badge. All these years. Does your boy know?"

Samantha tried harder to block him out, a tear leaking from behind her eyelids. But he oozed around her mental walls, stealing and putting filthy fingerprints on her memories.

"Or do you keep it in your car so he won't find it in your house? Oops, what house?" Morris said, grinning and brushing back hair that wasn't falling into his face. "Such pretty, pretty fires. Three blind mice going down, down into Abaddon."

Samantha steeled herself and sat back down. "Did you do it, Diego? Did you kill Danny and Isabel and Beth Sanford?"

Morris leaned backward. "There you go, Miranda, always blaming me for everything," he said cheerfully.

"If you didn't, then who did?" Samantha challenged. "You must know, as all-powerful as you are."

"Flattery is beneath you, Miranda," Morris said. "Ask the girl with the gray eyes and the secrets. Lovely little thing, she was. You were mean not to let me keep her." Morris whistled a little, still smiling.

"Celia," Freitas growled.

Samantha reached out and Morris slapped his still-bound hands over hers. The hideous cheer was gone from his face. His eyes burned with the mad glitter Samantha knew too well.

"Zorathenne," he said, his voice deeper as though commanding her. "Follow the fire down beneath Martin's blood. But there is more awaiting you, Samantha. You and Ryan and Drew. Do not go unprepared."

Then Morris slumped in his chair, muttering nonsense words over and over.

"What is Zorathenne?" Freitas wondered aloud.

Morris jumped up out of his chair. "Abaddon! Abaddon!" he shouted, kicking his chair over.

Dr. Hickerson leaped to his feet and tried to restrain him. "Jeff, it's okay! You're you again! It's okay—"

Morris swung his bound hands at Dr. Hickerson, knocking him away. Freitas moved to restrain him but Samantha and Ryan got there first. They held him still with vampire strength while Dr. Hickerson called for a sedative.

"Abaddon," Morris stammered again while they injected him. He made a small whimpering sound that cut through to Samantha's heart. She looked down on him as he looked up at her with sad, horrified eyes.

"I'm sorry," she whispered as the guards took him away.

Dr. Hickerson glared at her. "I should hope so. I don't suppose it matters to you people that you've set him back months."

"It matters to me," Samantha said in a small voice. "Thank you, Doctor."

"Don't give me any thanks," Dr. Hickerson snapped. "I'd have stopped you if I could."

"I don't mean for today," Samantha replied. "For what you're doing here. I hope you can help him and others like him. Thank you for what you do."

Dr. Hickerson didn't answer but his anger faded. Freitas led the way back out, picking up her notebook from the guard and immediately scribbling in it.

"What's Zorathenne?" she asked them as they went out to the car.

"No idea," Ryan replied, and Samantha shrugged as well.

"Abaddon?" Freitas asked.

Samantha thought for a moment. "I know it means the realm of the dead in ancient Hebrew, or a place of death and destruction."

"I thought it was the name of a demon, like *the* demon, a destroyer at Satan's right hand guarding the bottomless pit. Something very demonic," Ryan mused.

Samantha shook her head. "The occult was never really Diego's thing."

"Abaddon could just be referring to...to the ones who are dead, where they might be," Ryan said with difficulty. "To Diego, it would be fun to hint that Isabel and Danny are..."

"I'm dropping you two off at the club," Freitas interrupted. "I've got work to do."

* * * * *

Celia walked up the narrow stairs, pushing past a raving junkie who smelled like month-old gym socks and wore a ripped T-shirt extolling the virtues of oral sex. At the top of the stairs, she stepped over a passed-out human and walked down to the end of the hallway. She knocked on number 341.

"Come in," a hollow voice spoke.

Celia eased into the darkened room. "Hey," she said.

Lucas stood by the window, staring down at the blackened remains of the community center. Firefighters kept swarming around, chopping into the remnants of walls, hosing down still-steaming piles of debris.

"Danny helped me get this room," Lucas said. "Said it was a crappy hole in the wall but it beat the streets."

"Sort of," Celia said, stepping on a small roach as she came around the small bed to join him by the window. "It ain't the Ritz."

"Danny always saw the good stuff," Lucas said in that same hollow voice. "Told me I could even go to college, qualify for a grant or a scholarship or something, if only I could finish high school. He believed in me, yanno?"

Celia stepped up next to him. "Just 'cause Danny's dead don't make that stuff not true," she said, and Lucas flinched. "Not sayin' it don't make it go away either," she added.

"Is Samantha okay? Did you see her?" Lucas asked.

Celia shook her head. "Only Kelly. She's workin' the case, you know."

Lucas looked up at her, his eyes suddenly frightened.

"Don't worry," Celia reassured him. "I ain't gonna tell."

"Kelly's a cop, a good cop, and she don't look the other way when she sees something," Lucas insisted.

Celia folded her arms. "You gotta trust me, Lucas. I ain't saying a word. You just keep calm and everything'll be okay."

Lucas stared back down at the ruin of the community center. "Funny. In a situation like this, I'd go talk to Danny."

Celia followed his gaze. "I know what you mean," she said quietly.

* * * * *

Nocturnal Urges was closed when Samantha and Ryan returned. Brent let them in, his large, clumsy hand resting on Samantha's shoulder in intended comfort.

Robert Carton sat at a table alone in the empty club.

"He's been here for a couple of hours," Brent murmured.

Ryan squeezed Samantha's hand. "Do you want me to stay?"

Samantha shook her head and Ryan faded back to the anteroom with Brent. She took comfort knowing they were nearby as she approached the table.

"Hello, Robert," she said, sitting down with him.

Robert stirred a drink in which the ice had long since melted. "They're still cleaning it up," he said, and the sound of his broken voice rolled against her flimsy defenses. "I'm waiting. Hiding from the reporters. They said it'll be a while yet. Before they find the..."

The body. Samantha looked down at her hands. "Robert, you should try to get some sleep," she said quietly.

"Don't feel like it," Robert said in that horrid dead voice, stirring his drink some more. "For the first time, God forgive me, I'm glad his mother is dead. She couldn't have...have stood this. I'd be burying her too."

"I thought you—" Samantha stopped, horrified at what she was about to say. *I thought you didn't love her.*

Robert raised hooded eyes to her and she saw he knew exactly what had been on her mind. "I admit my mistakes, Samantha," he said. "I know what Danny must have thought of me. He hid it well."

"Danny," she began, and had to swallow past the lump in her throat before she could continue. Just saying his name cut her, twisted in her gut. "Danny respected you a great deal, Robert. He knew you were doing important things."

Robert stood and flung his drink across the club in a sudden, violent motion that made Samantha jump. The glass shattered against the stage where the band's equipment rested, spraying scotch whiskey onto the floor.

"I never did anything important!" he shouted. "My son was important! My s-son..." He shuddered and reached out for the chair. Samantha helped him back to the chair and waved back Brent, who had stuck his head in the main club room at the noise.

"So much I wanted to tell him and never did," Robert whispered.

Samantha lowered her eyes. "I know how you feel."

"Do you?" Robert snapped, and the venom in his voice made her flinch. "I warned him. I told him he was throwing his life away with you."

Samantha recoiled as if she had been struck. She'd known something had happened in the early months, the way Danny came to her one night tense and unsmiling and would not say what had been said.

"I loved Danny," she said with as much strength as she could muster. "I won't apologize for that."

"You loved a lot of men," Robert shot back.

Samantha was getting angry. "I seem to recall you didn't have to be dragged into this building, Mr. Carton," she retorted. "You didn't mind what I did when I was doing it with you."

"If it wasn't for you—" he began, and stopped.

If it wasn't for you, Danny would still be alive. Samantha felt as though he had said it, drilling through to her still heart like a cold bullet tearing into her.

Robert looked away and she felt it again, that pervading unease she had always felt with Danny's father. For Danny's sake, she had overcome it, in the name of peaceful family relations. For her sake, Danny had hid what Robert really thought of their relationship. For Danny's sake, Robert had hid it as well.

"So many lies," she whispered.

"I was afraid for Danny. I wanted him to have more than I could give him. He was my son," Robert said, his voice breaking again. "I wanted the world for him. I wanted more for him than...than this."

Abaddon

Robert's hands clenched and unclenched, and deep, shuddering sobs racked within him. Samantha felt his grief enveloping him and it reached out to overwhelm her. In a terrible, shuddering moment, her heart cried out for Danny, for his cheerful smile and comforting embrace. She wanted solace with him, the feel of him standing at her back, holding her close, giving her strength. She felt alone and exposed, adrift before Robert's agony.

Unbidden, her mind drifted to the night nearly a century ago when Cristoval sank his teeth into her neck and made her what she was. She hated Cristoval in that moment, with the same unreasoning, irrational anger that had made Robert strike out at her. She hated Cristoval for making her into this unnatural *thing* that destroyed all she touched.

For the first time, she longed for the bite, for the final kiss of night to send her on to whatever hell might wait for her.

Surely it could be no worse than this.

But the image of the scimitars intervened, the three swords crisscrossed on the wall in room four. The *Desafío* challenge. Justice first.

"You should get some sleep," she said again, standing up. The movement made her headache swell again, pounding behind her eyes.

Robert shook his head, not looking at her. "Not until they find my boy," he said brokenly, and her heart shattered again.

My boy. That's what Diego had called him. As though Danny were her pet, something she kept under her control to amuse her. For all Diego's supposed understanding of her, that was one thing his warped mind simply could not comprehend. There was no ownership with Danny, no battle of power and control to leverage between them. Danny did not possess her and she did not possess him. He was part of her and she of him. Not ownership. Belonging. The two shall become one body, one spirit, one soul, and all the nonsense in the world could not put them asunder.

Until death we do part.

Chapter Five
ಸಾ

December 16

Christopher called again. I am becoming worried about this continued contact. I enjoy his company. But I'm beginning to think he has more than friendship on his mind.

I can't deny it's an intoxicating idea. I honestly can't remember the last time Drew so much as looked in my direction, and here is this dashing young man, so fascinated by me. I really can't understand it. I'm not a beautiful woman, I wasn't even before the gray started to appear in my hair. Surely I must be reading too much into Christopher's attentions.

And Drew... I still love Drew. How could I not? He has not changed an iota since the day we met. He stays the same, handsome and brilliant, as I grow old beside him. I know there is much on his mind lately—it seems he is distracted, his thoughts elsewhere. Honestly, I sometimes wonder if he sees me at all. When we sit down to breakfast together, I want to wave my hand between his eyes and the newspaper beside his mug of blood, just to see if he'll notice.

The women's magazines all tell us to spice up our marriages in some dramatic manner. Go away on a trip together. Greet him at the door wearing slinky lingerie. I laugh at this—Drew would be utterly nonplussed if I wore black lace when he came home and I know he would never spare the time away from VAMP for a holiday.

Is this the way all marriages turn out? Two people moving in endless circles around each other, like moons caught in each other's gravitational pull, unable to come closer or pull apart. We are not married, but that is a technicality. I knew when I agreed to be his consort that I would grow old and die beside a man who will never age. I knew my heart would not change as time goes on. But I never thought his heart would fade as time went on.

I must admit, I wonder what Drew would think of Christopher's attentions. It is a foolish, cruel thought. If I cannot stir interest and affection in him, perhaps I can stir jealousy. Fortunately, these thoughts do not go any further than my imagination.

Christopher is coming to the house day after tomorrow to bring me yet another donation. I shall make it clear to him that our relationship is at most friendship. I hope Drew will be home. It will be better if he can finally meet Drew, to see that my consort is a real man, not some abstract encumbrance.

I hope he does not take it badly.

* * * * *

When the precinct door slammed, a framed award fell off the wall.

Parker strode across the squad room, her rage rolling off her in tangible waves. Detective Ken Henry actually scuttled out of her way, though he and Parker regarded each other with hot contempt on the best of days. Parker was just short of running, her stride strong and furious, and even Henry kept out of her way.

Parker slammed open the interrogation room door and didn't even pause for speaking. "Shut the hell up right now. This is over."

Freitas stood up, her arms folded. "Good morning, Parker."

Celia sat at the table, her hands folded in front of her, her spiky black hair more mussed than usual as her head bowed. Lieutenant Chris Cox stood over her, glaring at Celia and Parker with equal contempt.

"What the fuck do you think you're doing, interrogating a minor outside the presence of her guardian?" Parker shouted at them. "For that matter, what the fuck are you doing here at all, Anne? Jesus Christ, that's Celia sitting there!"

"Your ward has been named as a material witness in an open homicide investigation," Cox shot back. "We informed you she was being brought in, just as the regulations require."

"After you picked her up! Without giving her the chance to come in voluntarily!" Parker shouted. "I'm her legal guardian and as of right now, she declines to cooperate."

"You don't want that, Parker," Freitas said, shutting the door to block the curious faces peering from the squad room. "It's very bad for your career to be obstructing an investigation."

"You, I cannot fucking believe," Parker snapped at Freitas. "If you were interrogating the child of any cop in this department, you'd treat them with more respect than this."

"She's not your child," Cox snapped.

"Yes, she is!" Parker returned. "Foster parent. Look it up."

"I didn't say nothing," Celia said quietly.

Parker sat beside Celia. "Good. They know better. Did you Mirandize her?" She glared at Freitas, who stood stone-faced on the other side of the table. "Even if she knew anything, whatever she said would likely have been inadmissible, Anne. Jesus! Are you *trying* to fuck up this investigation?"

"Looks like you're the one fucking up the investigation," Cox shot back.

Parker stood, getting dangerously close to Cox's florid face. "Yeah, and beating the shit out of any vampire on the street is much more effective," she returned.

Cox pointed a finger in her face and Parker resisted the urge to smack it away. "I've about had it with your accusations, *Detective*," he snapped, emphasizing her rank. "My team is doing what needs to be done to handle the vampire problem in this city."

"The vampire *problem?* What exactly is the vampire problem, other than the fact that they exist?" Parker snapped.

"The bite mark on your neck shows you don't need a fuckin' slide show on the subject," Cox shot back. Reflexively, Parker's hand snapped up to cover the scar.

"Lieutenant, that's enough," Freitas interjected.

Parker turned away from Cox, staring at her partner. "What's your evidence of Celia's involvement?"

"Diego," Freitas said, and Cox glared at her.

Parker gritted her teeth. "He's back?"

"Hell no," Cox snapped. "We'd have him in chains for his goddamn execution."

Parker opened her mouth to say that the Chain Gang had had Diego once and let him get away, but the last shred of control in her anger stopped her. Diego had gotten away by killing four police officers under Cox's command. Cox was a son of a bitch of the first order. But cops don't needle other cops about losing fellow officers in the line of duty. There's a line a fellow officer doesn't cross.

"Diego specifically mentioned Celia, the 'one with the secrets'. We're just trying to find out what secrets he might be talking about," Freitas said.

"Motherfuck," Cox growled in frustration, stalking to the door. "Detective, come with me."

"I don't answer to you," Freitas snapped back.

"You called me with this!" Cox yelled. "I'm running the goddamn investigation, so until they bring in the fucking FBI, I'm lead investigator. Get your ass out here!"

Freitas stood toe to toe with Cox and was about to say something when Parker spoke up. "Both of you get the fuck out. I'm exercising my right to speak with my ward alone."

They both glared at her. Then Cox stalked out.

Parker spoke before Freitas could leave. "That means no listening in, Anne," she said. Freitas nodded without looking at her and stepped out, closing the door.

Parker exhaled. "Damn, Celia. What the hell have you gotten into now?"

Celia rolled her eyes. "I didn't do nothing. I don't know what the fuck they're talking about."

Parker didn't look at her, knowing Celia was more likely to freeze up with direct eye contact. "Cox is an asshole but Annie doesn't fuck around," she said. "She wouldn't bring you here without a good-faith basis for it."

"Thought you were pissed at her," Celia said.

Parker grimaced. "Damn straight. But pissed or not, she's a good cop. She believes you know something and that tells me you probably know something."

"I don't know nothing," Celia insisted.

"Could be Diego's just fucking with us," Parker said, and Celia flinched at Diego's name. "Sorry, kid," she said more quietly. "I know."

Celia stood and walked over to the tiny, barred window. "Don't matter none. Didn't hurt me."

"Then what secret is he talking about?" Parker asked.

Celia shrugged.

"You know something and it has to do with Danny and Isabel. No one's blaming you — well, no one sane is blaming you," Parker amended. "Whatever it is, you probably don't think it has anything to do with this."

Celia was mute, staring away from Parker.

Parker was starting to get angry. "You can pull that stone-faced shit in the dojo, I don't give a damn," she snapped. "But try to take just a second and think about Isabel and Danny. Remember them? Remember how Danny stood up for you against Diego, of all people? He didn't know fuck-all about you and still he stood between you and a goddamn crazy-ass vampire! Remember how Danny pulled strings to get you placed with me?"

Parker paused, staring at Celia, who stood resolutely silent. "Remember how many times Isabel helped you with your homework at the community center? Remember the journal she gave you? You do still have it, don't you? Didn't pawn it as soon as she was dead?"

As soon as she said it, she regretted it. The hurt was immediate on the girl's face, suddenly looking as young as she really was. Celia let out an incoherent cry and swung at Parker, who blocked it efficiently and caught the girl as she overbalanced. "Fuck you, fuck you, go to fuckin' hell," Celia cried, and her thin body shook.

For once, Parker didn't let go. She held Celia tightly, tears finally stinging her own eyes. "Who are you protecting, Celia?" she whispered into the girl's ear.

Celia pushed away from Parker and leaned against the cinderblock wall, her hand running over her spiky hair. "Lucas," she whispered, not looking up. "He's a vampire."

Parker's mouth dropped open in shock.

"He had his teeth fixed so he can't bite," Celia said. "He gets his blood at Nocturnal Urges, Andi and David sneak it to him. I figured it out when we fucked the first time."

"God, Celia…" Parker's voice trailed off.

Celia turned around, her large gray eyes hurt and angry at the same time. "He didn't do nothing," she said in a rush. "Not Isabel and sure-hell not Danny. He worshipped Danny. Danny was like a big brother to him, to all the guys at the center. He'd never hurt Danny. I know it wasn't him and that motherfuck out there would drag him away in silver chains if he knew. But it's…it's all I know."

Celia fell silent. Parker didn't know what to do or say. It was more words than Celia had ever said to her all at once, standing before the window and suddenly looking young, thin and vulnerable in a way she had never seemed before.

Outside, the shouting was getting louder. Celia jumped when the door banged open and Fradella stuck his head in. "Parker! You can take the girl home now."

"The fuck you say!" Cox shouted from behind him. "That's my suspect in there!"

"Not anymore!" Fradella yelled.

"Dammit, Frank..." Freitas began, but he cut her off.

"Go home, Detective," he said coolly. "You are off duty until your brain comes back. You are off this case for good."

Freitas stared at Fradella. Parker could read her silent pleading, *Please don't do this.* Fradella was trying to be impassive, the cop and the man warring with each other, but he did not relent. Parker silently screamed, wishing to be anywhere but here. Cox of course just fumed, totally oblivious.

"Parker, take the day." Fradella didn't look at her.

"Thanks, boss," Parker said, motioning to Celia. The teenager picked up her denim jacket and followed Parker, quiet. They walked out past the officers in the precinct who made no pretense of their interest, staring at them.

"What now?" Celia whispered as they left the building.

"You and me, we're gonna go talk to Lucas," Parker said, going to her car. "Diego had a reason to point us toward him."

"We're takin' orders from Psycho Boy now?" Celia asked. "'Cause I really don't feel like a repeat performance from his crazy ass."

"You and me both," Parker said tiredly, leaning against her car. Unconsciously she rubbed the scar on her neck.

Celia stared at her. "Did he... I mean, I heard he hurt you," she said tentatively.

Parker raised her gaze to Celia's gray eyes. There was a touch of concern there, something more human than she'd ever seen behind the wall Celia had always kept between them. "Just a bite," she said. "The mind-touch was worse."

"It's supposed to feel good," Celia said quietly.

Parker shook her head. "If they make it that way," she said carefully. "Diego…he didn't like it that way."

Celia leaned against the car beside her, staring up at the sky. "You really think Lucas knows something?"

"Or Diego's just fucking with us," Parker said. "I put nothing past him. And I've been reading something rather interesting in Beth Sanford's journal. That's why we need to–"

"Need to talk to me," Freitas finished, walking up to them.

Parker glared at her partner. "Annie, you really don't want to be around me right now," she snapped. "I'm this close to asking the lieutenant for a goddamn transfer. I cannot believe you did this."

"I had to," Freitas said. "Diego—"

"Yeah, you wanna fill me in on that?" Parker asked. "What the hell does Diego have to do with this? Did you get a note from him stating 'Killer This Way'? And start with why the fuck you didn't call me about it?"

Freitas glanced over her shoulder, quiet for a moment. Then she began to speak, telling them about the trip to the Wallsh Institute, about Jeff Morris and Samantha. "He said a lot of crazy shit that I don't understand," she said. "But Celia, that part was easy. I have to know what she knows."

"You missed the part where you tell *your partner* about it," Parker snapped. "Especially since you're talking about Celia!"

"I know," Freitas sighed quietly.

Parker was about to launch into another rant but Freitas' quiet agreement derailed her. "Well."

"I'm…y'know," Freitas said, avoiding eye contact.

Parker stared at her.

"If you two are done," Celia snarked. "She can come with us."

Parker blinked. "Are you sure?"

Celia shrugged. "Two cops're better'n one. 'Cept asswipe upstairs."

Parker smothered a slight grin.

* * * * *

The door to Vampires Against Mortal Perversion was adorned with a simple black wreath, wound through with white roses. It contrasted sharply with the cheerful Christmas decorations throughout the high-rise in which Drew Sanford's group worked. The Christmas tree in the lobby shone with sparkling gold and burgundy decorations, and cheerful carols rang through the hallways.

The windows of the office behind the wreath were dark save one. *Closed,* read a discreet sign under the wreath.

Ryan knocked anyway. Samantha stood behind him, listless. Neither of them had been able to sleep much and Fiona had finally threatened to have Brent hold them down and force-feed them if they didn't drink some blood. It tasted bitter.

Ryan knocked again and finally the door swung open. A young-looking vampire woman in a somber black suit answered, her eyes reddened. "We're closed, sir," she said quietly. "There's been a death—"

"I know," Ryan interrupted. "Tell Mr. Sanford that Ryan Callahan is here."

The woman shook her head sadly. "Mr. Sanford is seeing no one until Beth...his consort is buried," she said.

Ryan leaned toward her. "Tell him Ryan Callahan is here about Abaddon."

She blinked but the look on his face must have convinced her. She disappeared into the darkness of the office and Ryan and Samantha stepped into the shadowed foyer. There were a few boxes of Christmas decorations on the floor—the office had apparently been decorated for the holidays and the blonde woman had been taking them down when they arrived. Samantha suddenly remembered it was supposed to be the Christmas season. Peace on Earth, goodwill toward men. And women. But not vampires.

She shook her head, trying to clear the empty bitterness that seemed to be overtaking her. She felt numb, truly dead inside and out, as though nothing would move her or touch her again except the dull headache behind her eyes.

Ryan, however, seemed lit by a new fire. Something was driving him far beyond what she felt capable of feeling. He literally could not keep still, constantly shifting his weight and moving around the room. It was exhausting just to watch him.

"He'll see you," the blonde woman said from the hallway, beckoning to them. Samantha followed Ryan down the hallway to Drew Sanford's office, discreetly marked *Executive Director*.

The office was as dark as the rest of the rooms. When the blonde woman stepped out, closing the door, it took Samantha's eyes a moment to adjust to the darkness.

Drew Sanford swung around in his chair. The change in his face was marked. He had always been a slim man but now he was pale and gaunt with circles under his eyes. *He's starving himself,* Samantha thought.

"You have no business in this," Drew said without preamble. "Stay away from it. Bury your loved ones and go on with your lives."

"The hell you say," Ryan shot back. "Have you even eaten since you left the hospital?"

"I do not recall us being close friends, Mr. Callahan," Drew said in his cool, dry voice. "As a matter of fact, I recall more than a few jibes tossed my way when I was on the protest line in front of that cesspool you call a workplace. Therefore your concern is entirely misplaced."

"It doesn't appear whoever's doing this cares much which of us is right about the bite and which is wrong," Ryan said.

"Neither do they care much for human life. Personally, I mean to do something about it and we have a few clues. Abaddon for example. You know what it means."

"I know what it means, you're mispronouncing it and that's the end of the conversation," Drew said.

Ryan blinked.

"Ah-bah-*dunn*," Drew said, over-pronouncing as if speaking to a particularly slow child.

"Damn Diego anyway," Ryan muttered.

"We know it has something to do with whoever killed Isabel, Beth and D-Danny," Samantha said, her heart twisting at the names. The two men flinched as well and Ryan seized on it.

"Think about Beth," Ryan said, leaning forward to rest his hands on Drew's desk. "You were unconscious when he killed her."

"Be silent," Drew said, but his voice held no command.

"Were you awake at all?" Ryan needled. "Unable to move, unable to think but slightly aware, knowing there was something horrible happening just beyond? The smell of the smoke. The sound of the sirens. You lay there helpless while he entered your home and attacked your consort, the one you swore to protect at the cost of your own life."

Drew's hands clenched on the armrests of his chair. Samantha wanted to tell Ryan to stop, to leave him alone, but even that seemed to be beyond her in this deadened state.

"Nothing will bring Beth back to me," Drew said quietly.

"So that's it? Just let the son of a bitch go?" Ryan challenged. "Doesn't look like that decision is sitting too well with you, Drew. Personally, I'm having the damnedest time trying to sleep. Must be Isabel screaming inside my head."

Samantha's headache was suddenly much, much worse. It pounded inside her skull as though there were a huge swelling balloon inside her skull, filled with blood. She wanted to plead with Ryan to stop, to let Drew alone. She tried to block out the pain, tried to stop from feeling anything. Instead, the pulsing flames seemed to lick behind her eyes, as though the heat from the fire that had consumed Danny was now contained inside her head.

"Samantha?" Ryan said, but she couldn't answer.

"Zorathenne," she murmured, and the image rose inside her head, a woman of dark, cold beauty, standing... She staggered a little and Ryan slid an arm around her shoulders, steadying her. The image faded but the pain remained strong, settling into her head and making her sick to her stomach.

"Take two aspirin, Ms. Crews," Drew replied. "You want no part of this."

Samantha raised her eyes with difficulty to glare at him. "They killed Danny!" she cried, and the tears began to well up again. "How can you sit there and do nothing! Was your consort so meaningless to you? So worthless? You were together for decades, and you can simply cast her aside as though she were nothing?"

Drew spoke with difficulty. "I have outlived nine consorts in my lifetime, Ms. Crews. Eternal life is a cruel mistress. It is a loss with which I am all too familiar."

"How many were murdered?" Ryan snapped, still steadying Samantha. "How many were viciously attacked while you lay nearby, useless to her?"

Drew suddenly bolted to his feet. "Shut up!" he shouted, and the vehemence startled Ryan and Samantha. Then he seemed to recover himself, leaning on the chair and speaking in a quieter voice. "There is no way to challenge..."

"The challenge," Samantha said, her head swelling in pain. "The *Desafío*."

Drew was already shaking his head. "You have gone completely mad. The *Desafío* is of another time. There are few vampires who even remember the old challenge exists."

"Not that much to it," Samantha retorted. "A ceremonial weapon, a declaration of vengeance and the fight."

"Which you would surely lose," Drew returned.

"Watch me," Ryan countered, his face grim. "Come with us or don't. It's your choice. What we need from you is information. What is Abaddon?"

Drew sat back down again, slowly. "It is where *they* are. They are old, older than most of the city itself," he said.

"Vampires?" Ryan asked.

Drew nodded. "Ancient, deadly. And quite mad. I did mention that part, didn't I? They were already ancient during the Inferno of 1873, when the humans burned so many of us in the streets. That's when the name came into being, at least— *Abaddon*, a reference to the angel guarding the bottomless pit in hell. Appropriate, no?"

Samantha closed her eyes, leaning on Ryan. "Another kiss gone insane. This is getting old."

Drew steepled his fingers in front of him. "Not quite like a kiss," he said. "It's similar. But stronger and weaker. Imagine a kiss composed of vampire leaders, each with his or her own followers. A kiss with greater autonomy but bit by bit taking over the entire city's vampire following."

Ryan shook his head. "Then why? Why Isabel? Or Beth or Danny? They're humans."

"Humans living with vampires," Drew said quietly. "They believe humans are food, nothing more. They consider our decision to mate with them and make them consorts to be perversion, something on the level of bestiality."

"My God," Samantha whispered, staring at Ryan. "What if Diego has joined with them?"

Ryan held out a hand to Drew. "Come with us," he said. "It should be all three of us. We'll have a better chance with you."

Drew shook his head. "I am no fighter and I have no idea where to find them," he said. "I am no use to you."

"Diego said we had to follow 'the fire below Martin's blood'," Ryan said. "Now, I've got no idea what the hell His Royal Lunacy is talking about but I bet you do, and if he says we need you, then I guess we need you."

Drew was still, staring at Ryan. "Martin's blood?" he asked, his voice suddenly shaky. "That's it?"

Samantha's headache eased a bit.

* * * * *

Fiona was royally pissed. She stood with her hands on her hips, glaring at the three of them. "And just suppose I tell you no?" she shouted at Ryan, a touch of Irish brogue coming out in her voice that Samantha had never heard before. "You can't have the scimitars, and if you go on with this plan, aye, I'll put the cops on you!"

"Then I quit," Ryan said easily, taking the third scimitar down from the wall of room four and handing it to Samantha.

"Fine!" Fiona snapped. "At least you'll be alive!"

Samantha stood beside Drew, who looked as if he were resisting the urge to hide behind the furniture. He had protested having to enter the club he abominated. "Something tells me the word Abaddon isn't entirely new to you, Fiona," she said.

Fiona flinched. "You of all people need to stay the hell away from *that*," she said. "Once they get a taste of that lovely power in your head, dearie, you'll never see daylight again."

"Not happening," Ryan said, testing the edge of a scimitar. "Brent, do you have a polishing cloth or whetstone? These things have been on the wall too long."

Brent vanished into the back, past Fiona's furious glare.

"How about instead of vague warnings, you tell us the truth?" Samantha asked Fiona. "Do you know of Abaddon? Do you know why they killed Danny? Is Diego with them?"

Fiona swept over to Samantha, ignoring Brent's return as he and Ryan polished the swords. She placed her hands on Samantha's shoulders. "I've known you since you were made, dear," she said softly, with an almost motherly tone to her usually stern voice. "I've watched you grow more powerful than even Cristoval and he was the strongest vampire I'd ever known. You fought Diego to a standstill. But I'm not just worried about your safety. I'm worried about that power in your mind. With you in Abaddon, they'd come up to the city. The humans couldn't stop them. It'd be the Inferno all over again, only with us against the humans."

"Since when do you care about lowly humans?" Samantha sniped, but she was being unfair and she knew it.

Fiona ignored her comment. "Think of something beyond your pain, Samantha," she said quietly. "Would Danny want you to risk such a disaster in his name? Blood in the streets? Is that the way to celebrate his life?"

Samantha almost faltered. The image of blood flowing down the broken pavement made her heart hurt. But it mixed with the memory of filthy water cascading down from the community center, flowing over her as she screamed. All that she and Danny had built together, gone in the same blaze that had taken him from her. Her headache was back again, roiling against her eyes and temples.

"The humans caused this," she said bitterly. "They were the ones who drove us underground, who keep us tied down under their heels. They rejected us and anyone who loved us. Let them burn."

Fiona recoiled, uncertainty and sadness in her face.

"Let them burn! Let them all burn!" Samantha shouted in Fiona's face and Ryan moved beside her, placing a steadying hand on her shoulder as she fought down the tears yet again.

The door to room four opened and a tall man with reddish hair stuck his head in, holding up a badge. "Excuse me, Jon Flanigan with the state fire marshal's office," he said by way of introduction, his voice faltering at the glares from the vampires. "I'm...looking for Samantha Crews?" His eyes fell on Samantha first then stared at the scimitars on the bed. "Can I ask what those are for?"

"Very busy, just leaving," Ryan snapped, gathering up the scimitars. Ryan, Samantha and Drew walked past Flanigan, who tried to step in front of them.

Brent stepped in front of Flanigan, his eyes flaring. Flanigan tried to shout after Samantha as she left the room.

Brent shoved him up against the wall, hissing.

"*LEAVE HER ALONE*," Brent commanded, and Flanigan immediately fell silent, caught by Brent's eyes.

"Brent! Back down!" Fiona cried, but for once Brent didn't answer. She shouted into the air. "Zorathenne! Damn you, let him go!"

The fury in Brent's eyes eased and he stepped back immediately.

"My apologies, sir," Fiona said smoothly.

"Goddammit," Flanigan said, stumbling away and shaking his head. "That was...Samantha Crews."

"Yes, and she doesn't need *your kind* bothering her right now," Fiona replied coolly.

"Oh God," Brent whispered. "I'm so sorry...go, stop her..." Fiona whirled to see a look of horror spreading across Brent's face.

"What? What is it?" Fiona asked.

Flanigan was already fumbling for his cell phone as he ran out to the parking lot.

* * * * *

Parker's car screeched as she tore through the streets. "Annie, put up the bubble," she ordered, driving one-handed with the cell phone held to her ear. For once, Freitas simply did it without arguing.

"What the hell?" Celia asked, bracing herself in the backseat.

"Flanigan's following Samantha, Ryan and Drew Sanford," Parker said, still listening to directions on her cell phone. "He thinks they're gonna do something stupid. They've got weapons and they gave him the slip at the club."

"We should call Cox," Freitas said, and immediately regretted it.

Parker gave her an "are you fucking stupid" look. "You ever want to see them again?"

"Maybe we should leave them alone," Celia offered from the backseat. "They got a right."

Parker wasn't listening, her ear glued to her phone. Her car swerved to the side and Freitas shouted something incoherent as Parker barely kept them from running off the road.

"Holy shit," Parker whispered.

"What? What is it?" Freitas asked, bracing herself on the dashboard.

"Danny," Parker said, stunned. "Flanigan says they finally got the hot spots out and dug through the whole community center, what's left of it. Danny's body isn't there."

Celia gaped. "But Lucas saw him! Danny went into the building and never came out!"

Freitas stared over the back of the seat at Celia. "Tell me about Lucas."

* * * * *

Saint Bartholomew's Church rose before them, the sun beginning to set behind the skyscrapers and the skeletons of winter-bare trees, casting a serene glow against the church's white marble and granite. Its lovely red doors were unlocked, allowing the passersby to enter the white citadel for reflection and prayer.

Three vampires strode in the front door and down the long marble aisle, scimitars in hand. Ryan and Drew both genuflected before the cross above the altar, lit with its own warm yellow glow. Samantha remained resolutely still.

Father Stubblefield entered from the parish hall and stopped, frozen at what he saw.

All three dipped their fingers in the font of holy water, almost in defiance of silly myths banning them from all things holy. They made the sign of the cross on their foreheads, touching the swords each carried with a drop of sacred water.

Samantha turned to stare up at the stoic eyes of the saints, frozen in glorious beauty in the stained-glass windows surrounding them. Her gaze was not friendly.

Drew led them to the right of the altar, past the organ, down a few short steps to a curved, narrow hallway cut into the stone behind the altar.

Directly behind the altar was the window of Martin's Blood. There in century-old stained glass, a dark man writhed in agony as cloaked humans danced around the flames consuming him. His blood flowed from the fire down to the bottom of the window.

Etched beneath it were the words *His blood is upon us forever*.

"The Inferno," Drew whispered. "When the humans came for us with torches and hate. They burned him alive on the steps of this very church."

Ryan touched the window gently. "Were you there?"

Drew dropped his gaze. "I was nearby," he said. "I could not...help."

Samantha knelt before the window. Below it was a small wooden door about four feet tall. On it was engraved a pattern like flames and the small lock was old and dusty.

She struck the lock once with her scimitar. The lock snapped in two, falling to the floor with a clunk. The door swung open in a puff of gray dust, revealing a narrow passage leading straight down into unrelieved void.

Samantha looked up at the other two. "Time to dance with the devil."

Chapter Six

ಶು

December 18

Drew just called. He'll be late for our meeting with Christopher tonight. There is always a crisis.

On nights like tonight as I watch the snow fall outside our home, I remember when I first met Drew. He was hiding in a coffee shop in midtown. It was supposed to be a cloudy day but the sun had come out and he had forgotten his hat. The hippies were singing songs of peace, love, drugs and sex with bad guitar accompaniment and I was with them in my bellbottoms and ironed-straight hair. I sincerely hope I have burned all photos from that time.

He was so serious, so dedicated. I was the cheerful, carefree one then. My goodness, I was so young. I tried to teach him how to relax, how to have fun. He even smiled and I made him laugh a few times.

When did it go so quiet between us?

The other night Drew had a nightmare. He has only had perhaps nine or ten nightmares in all the years we've been together. He cried out in his sleep, a name like Zeela or something. I would be jealous, except he sounded so afraid, so sad. I tried to wake him but he would not stir. He fell quiet but his eyes have been haunted ever since. What can be dragging at his heart so? And why can't he tell me about it?

Christopher will be here any moment. I had so hoped Drew would be with us. But I suppose I will have to have my conversation with him alone. I hope I am wrong and we can laugh it off as a silly misunderstanding. Then Drew will arrive and join us and we will share a glass of wine by the fire as friends. And when Christopher leaves, I will make Drew leave his papers by his computer in the den. No late-night news, no radio, no phone calls. It has been literally years since we curled up in front of the fire.

Looking back over the last few weeks, I am ashamed of myself for this whole Christopher business. On the outside, I have done nothing inappropriate. But I would be lying if I said I was not at all intrigued by his attentions. It is a silly old — or middle-aged — woman's fancy and it is wrong.

I love Drew with all my heart, body, mind and soul. I have devoted my life to him and to our work together, and if I had to go back in time to that coffee shop as he hid from the sunlight, I would make the same choice again. And again and again and again. Until death do us part.

* * * * *

Samantha stepped slowly, listening for the footfalls of the two vampires behind her. The darkness was absolute. *Someone should have brought a flashlight,* she thought. They had dropped down from the wooden doorway into a narrow stone passageway and Drew had shut the door behind them, sealing them in darkness.

Step-by-step she inched along. It felt as if they were going downward at a steep angle. The air was cold and growing colder, dank and tasteless against her face.

The darkness was like something tangible, pressing against her. She needed to concentrate but the darkness was not her friend. Her eyes played tricks with her. Unable to see anything, her imagination played images from memory. She saw Danny's face over and over, as though he floated ahead of her, drawing her down the passageway.

Danny.

She saw his face, sad and yet loving in the cool moonlight on his porch. The last time she had seen him, and all he wanted was a promise from her that one day soon she would be with him, really be with him in body, mind and soul. All he wanted from her was the reassurance that her love was forever, as binding as his, and she couldn't give it to him.

Oh dear God, Danny, I'm so sorry. If only I'd known.

That was the problem with eternal life, she thought as she moved down the passageway. Living forever meant unlimited second chances. If she didn't visit the jazz club on Bourbon Street in New Orleans, surely it would be there when next she came to town, no matter how many decades and disasters might pass between visits. Surely the impressive skyline of New York City would remain unchanged in her long, long life, so why hurry to view it from the top of a skyscraper? The patterns of life grew long and as much as things changed, they still stayed the same. People breathed and laughed, fought and died, and nothing changed. Until of course they change, until a building falls and the water rushes in and suddenly everything is different, chances missed, opportunities lost.

Why tell her man how much he meant to her when surely he would always be at her side?

She should have known better.

Perhaps Ryan was right and she had no right to have loved Danny in the first place. Her heart wrenched as Robert's face replaced Danny's in the darkness in front of her. His face was harsh and accusing—*If it weren't for you, Danny would still be alive.*

It was true. She knew it was true. Was Diego so wrong? Was she nothing but a predator, a killer at heart?

Her foot slipped and she lurched through the air. The ground seemed to disappear beneath her and her startled cry failed to warn Ryan and Drew. She heard them yell as they tumbled through the darkness into...

Splash. The water was cold, almost unbearably so. The weight of the scimitar tied to her belt dragged at Samantha and she struggled to stay afloat. But it pulled at her and her arms grew tired.

"Ryan!" she cried, before the water dragged her under.

It was still completely black but almost peaceful. Samantha drifted downward, no longer trying to fight it. The scimitar's weight pulled her down almost endlessly, the water

Abaddon

drifting around her. It seemed like forever but could only have been moments until she struck bottom.

The moment her foot struck the stones on the bottom, the water lit up around her. A subtle fluorescence filled the water and she saw the large lever at the bottom of the huge water tank that disappeared into murky shadows in all directions. To her side, she saw Ryan landing less than gracefully on the bottom, which was stone covered with some kind of greenish moss.

Samantha trudged across the bottom of the tank toward the lever, walking almost in slow motion. It was harder than she thought it would be to move with the scimitar weighing her down. She realized if she had needed to breathe, she would have had to relinquish it in order to turn the lever.

It was old and rusted and it took all her strength to pull it. Once she did, however, there was a sudden roar and the water rushed from the chamber. They waited patiently as it flowed past them and out through a hidden sluice. When her head broke the surface, Samantha wiped the water from her eyes.

"Did you enjoy your swim?" asked Drew, perched above them on the ledge off which they had fallen.

"Some help you are," Ryan groused, shaking water out of his hair.

Samantha pointed to the far side of the deep chamber where a small door was recessed into the corner, far away from the lever. "Better jump while there's water to cushion your fall," she told Drew. "That's where we're going."

* * * * *

"I'll be damned," Parker said, leaning over the small doorway.

"At the very least," said Father Stubblefield wryly, examining the broken lock. "I do believe Father Cole told me that was just an old storage cabinet, no longer used, God rest his soul."

135

"That window gives me the creeps," Celia said, staring at Martin's Blood.

Flanigan came around the curve of the passageway behind the altar. He had three flashlights, a small box and a length of rope in hand. "Boy Scout motto," he said.

"What the hell is that?" Parker asked, pointing to the box.

"Basic first-aid kit," Flanigan said.

Parker shook her head. "Total Boy Scout."

"Be prepared," he said, handing flashlights to Freitas and Parker. "Always carry three light sources. Of course, they usually mean three sources *each*."

"Excuse me, but shouldn't we call more police?" Father Stubblefield asked.

Parker and Freitas stared at each other. "Do you really want Cox to get his hands on them?" Parker asked.

"They haven't committed a crime," Freitas said quietly.

"They will," Flanigan argued. "You didn't see them at the club. They were like the Three Musketeers or something."

"They got a right," Celia said again.

Parker turned to Celia. "You're staying with Father Stubblefield."

"No fuckin' way!" Celia shouted, and the priest flinched.

Parker stood firm in the girl's angry face. "We need backup," she said. "We need someone to get help if we get stuck somewhere and can't make it back."

"Bullshit," Celia shot back. "You think I'm a kid and I can't handle it. I can handle anything you can handle! Lucas is in this and I need to go with you!"

"We don't have time for this!" Freitas snapped. "Kid, you stay with the priest and get help if we're not back in two hours. We've only got the three flashlights, so three people are going and we're the only certified emergency responders here, got it?"

Celia glared at them both.

Parker pitched her voice low. "If you want to be treated like an adult, act like one," she said quietly.

That seemed to work where nothing else had. Celia stepped over by the priest, mutiny still clear in her crossed arms.

"That was fun," Flanigan said. "I think I'll go into the dark tunnel now, if that's okay with you brave cops."

"Sure," Parker said. "The monsters can get you first."

* * * * *

Torches set in cobwebby holders along the passageway had been lit, as though someone were waiting for them. The thought did not make Ryan happy.

The stone passageway must have taken them well beyond the limits of the Saint Bartholomew grounds. In fact, at the rate they seemed to be going down, Ryan was amazed they hadn't hit the high Memphis water table yet.

Ahead of him, Samantha's hand drifted to her temple again. Ryan could swear she was getting paler by the hour, even in the flickering torchlight. He had no real link to Samantha, but he needed none to see that she was in real physical pain beyond the emotional devastation of losing Danny.

But that made him think of Isabel, cold and white beneath the harsh fluorescent lights of the morgue. He had needed to see her, needed to know in his heart that she really was gone. But that was nonsense born of wishful thinking. He had known from the moment he awoke at the hospital that something was missing, that vital link snapped and left broken and raw.

Now he wished he had left well enough alone so he could remember Isabel dancing in the glow of the firelight. If he concentrated hard enough, he could remember the curve of her waist beneath his hand, beneath the soft burgundy velvet of her dress. Her smile as he dipped her before the fire, the glow of the flames dancing in her eyes. The way she had taken the Santa hat off her head as he opened the ring box, the way her hair had fallen around her face as she said yes, she would be his consort. The feel of her soft hand as he slipped the ring on her finger and the kiss they had shared before their friends, before the fire. He would remember the pounding drums of that last song for the rest of his life, the lyrics haunting him until his death, which he fervently hoped would be soon.

Ahead of them, the passage widened past yet another torch. Samantha stopped and Ryan looked over her shoulder.

"What is it?" asked Drew from behind him.

The chamber ahead was huge, impossibly so. The floor was difficult to see, vanishing into shadows beyond the flickering torchlight. Ahead of them, a large stone slab spanned the chasm. On the far side was a flat wall.

"Fee fie foe fum," Ryan muttered, and Samantha almost smiled. "Think there's another passage over there?"

"Let's go," she said.

Slowly they edged out onto the slab. It was flat and wide but there were no railings or handholds to keep them from tumbling off the edge. They moved together and Ryan rested his hand on his scimitar, just in case.

When all three had stepped onto the slab, there was a sudden groaning sound, a creaking scrape that set Ryan's teeth on edge. The slab tilted backward, the far end rising up toward the ceiling.

"Shit!" Ryan yelled, grabbing Samantha's hand. "Jump for it!"

Drew leaped straight back up to the ledge they had just left. When his weight left the slab, it settled back just below where it had been.

Ryan tested the stone beneath them, deceptively firm. "Damn."

"It's a teeter-totter," Samantha said. "Like the playground toy."

Drew blew out his breath in frustration. "This is getting very old," he snapped. "I'm tired of being played with!"

"You and me both," Ryan murmured, glancing over the side. He could not see the mechanism beneath them. "Stay here."

"Ryan," Samantha protested, but he was already moving across the slab alone.

As though it mattered what happened to him, he thought. If this little venture killed him, he would be well pleased. After all, he was already dead.

He had died a little the night Elyse woke as a vampire and began screaming, horrified by the monster he had made her become, refusing to believe that she truly had become a vampire. As a human she had loved him, but was sadly sure he was going to hell, as her church had taught her. He loved her and could not stand idly by and watch as she died. He did what he could and it was the mistake he would regret the rest of his life. He died when she whispered through tears that he had damned her to hell with him. He died a little more the day she was dragged into court to give testimony against him, still protesting her humanity, condemning him for "murdering" her. He died yet more the day he murdered her for real, killing her to save her the humiliation of a human trial and execution, mourning her and the men she had killed in her insanity. The insanity he had caused.

The slab moved a little beneath him and he moved faster to the midpoint.

He had been alive again with Isabel. In more than a century of living, he had had only a tiny span with Isabel — warm, brave Isabel, who had loved him for what he was, for everything he ever had been and everything he ever would be, who had risked everything she had to be with him. She had seen not only the man he was but the man he wanted to become. And for a brief time, he had been that man.

She had been taken from him. The cold fire had destroyed her and him along with her. The thought of returning to the unlife he had lived all those years before her was unbearable. He did not want to see daylight again.

But death would have to wait until he had ripped out the heart of Isabel's murderer.

Past the midpoint, Ryan felt the slab begin to tilt the other way this time, down beneath his feet and away from them. Samantha leapt back onto the far side and it settled.

"Stay there!" he shouted, edging toward the far wall.

It was completely solid. No button, no lever, no secret compartment. Nothing but a blank stone wall, mocking him in its solidity.

Ryan suddenly had an idea. He stepped backward a little. "Samantha, step off!" he shouted.

"Are you sure?" Drew called back.

"Yes!" Ryan replied.

Samantha stepped back onto the ledge with Drew. The slab tilted down away from them—and became a slide. Ryan fell straight down, slipping down the slab as it lowered…

To an open doorway. He tumbled through it onto hard stone. As soon as his weight was off the slab, it lifted back up without him.

"Do it!" Ryan shouted. "Trust me!"

Above him, the slab began to move.

* * * * *

"Christ!" Flanigan shouted, struggling through the hip-deep water. "What the fuck is this?"

"Could have been worse!" Freitas shouted back, pointing past Parker to the walls. "Look at the marks on the walls. This room is usually full up to there."

Flanigan stared up at the watermarks on the walls. "Damn. We'd have drowned."

"Speak for yourself," Parker said. "I can swim."

"Is there anything you can't do?" Flanigan asked, and she grinned. Freitas started to speak but Parker shot her a look and she subsided.

They trudged through the water, Freitas and Parker holding their weapons up in the air. "Is this the only way out?" Parker asked, looking at the door.

Flanigan shrugged. "You're looking at me? I've never been here before."

Parker smiled a little. "Silly me. Shall we?"

"What the hell," Freitas said, shoving the door open.

* * * * *

Samantha was in the lead when the bridge snapped beneath her.

The bridge was a simple wooden suspension across yet another miniature chasm. It had seemed simple enough—cross the bridge to the ornate carved wood door. Flickering torches set on either side of the door seemed to provide plenty of light.

Then a single wrong step and the wood broke easily beneath her.

"Shit!" Samantha shouted, grasping outward for anything she could hold to support her weight. Her legs fell through the new hole, her hands sliding down the wooden planks, garnering her little fire pricks of splinters on her palms.

"Samantha!" she heard Ryan shout from above as she struggled to hold on. The board supporting her upper torso snapped as well and just as she fell, Ryan grabbed her wrist.

Her weight pulled him down to his knees. "Hold on!" Ryan shouted, slipping toward the new hole in the bridge.

Samantha dangled there, unable to reach anything. Ryan was lying full-out on the bridge, his hand slipping from her wrist. Drew was trying to climb over him to offer his support.

"Watch out!" Samantha shouted, just before Drew put his foot on another cracked plank. From the underside, she could see several planks had been hinged—they didn't break after all, they were just designed to give way underfoot.

And the one under Ryan was starting to bend. He could feel it, she knew, and still he tried to reach down with his other hand, to pull her up.

She twisted her wrist and immediately he lost his grasp.

It was a shorter fall than she figured it would be. She landed on the stone floor a bare second later and her side took the brunt of the impact. She tested her arms and legs—everything worked, though she imagined her hip would be more than a little bruised.

Ryan and Drew were shouting. They couldn't see her in the shadows. "I'm all right!" she shouted back up. "Stupid booby trap! Nothing to it."

"If we make it out of here alive, I'm gonna kill you!" Ryan shouted back. "Next time I try to save you, let me!"

Samantha muttered something unkind under her breath as she looked around. On the far side of the stone chamber was a small, unassuming door with an arched top, tucked under the shadow of the bridge.

"Ryan, don't go to the big door!" Samantha called. "There's a door down here, I bet it's the way out!"

"Great," Drew groused, looking around. "And how do we get down?"

"Jump carefully," Samantha suggested.

Ryan jumped first through the hole Samantha had made in the bridge. He landed hard but kept his balance. Drew overbalanced and landed on his rear, letting out a curse that would have made his flock turn, well, paler. Samantha blinked.

As their weight left the bridge there was a click and the wooden panels that had opened beneath Samantha snapped back up into place.

"Really stupid," Ryan said. "That fall's no more than fifteen feet, shadows or no. Unlikely it would even kill a human, much less us."

Samantha looked around the chamber but other than some fairly good-sized holes and gaps in the masonry, there was nothing of import on the floor. She carefully tested a few stones with her foot but nothing happened.

"Hmmm," she said. "Onward, I guess."

Samantha tested the knob on the plain wooden door. It opened easily.

* * * * *

Freitas stood in the center of the giant stone slab as Parker and Flanigan balanced on either end. Flanigan was heavier and so the slab tilted a bit toward him.

"This is fucking stupid!" Freitas shouted in frustration. "What the hell are we supposed to accomplish?"

"Getting the fuck out of here and waiting in the cathedral for the Three Musketeers to come back on their own?" Flanigan offered.

"Fine, you go back through the nice dark passageways," Parker called. "Have fun swimming through Lake Memphis."

The slab tilted a bit more toward Flanigan. "There's a trick to this," he called.

"Maybe we're supposed to balance it perfectly?" Parker replied.

"Yeah!" Flanigan said. "Detective, go a bit farther toward Kelly."

Freitas moved backward on the slab, shifting her weight toward Parker at the end of the slab nearest the entrance. The slab moved up a bit under Flanigan, balancing flat.

Freitas looked around.

"Nothing's happening," she groused.

"Maybe one way or the other?" Flanigan suggested. "Detective, go back toward Parker. Then you both step off."

Freitas glared at him. "I cannot express the true stupidity of that idea," she said. "Likely you'll get squished flat by the giant stone."

Flanigan shrugged. "Then at least we'll know that's not what we're supposed to do."

"Very funny," Freitas grumbled, moving back toward Parker. As the two of them stepped back into the tunnel, the slab immediately tilted up and away from them and Flanigan disappeared from sight with a thump. Then his voice floated to them through the chamber.

"Whoa."

* * * * *

Celia perched on the edge of the small couch, her arms folded in her best snotty-teenager mode. The priest's office was small and warm, with woven rugs and framed prints of classic Biblical paintings above the bookshelves.

"Are you sure I can't offer you something?" Father Stubblefield said rather desperately.

Celia glared at him. "Fine, I'll take a soda."

Stubblefield gratefully crossed to the small dorm-style refrigerator, below a shelf full of heavy antiques and framed manuscripts of ancient texts. "I know how worried you must be about your foster mother," he said, leaning over to retrieve a soda can. "I must say, I think you're handling it very—"

Thud. Celia smacked the priest on the back of his head with a large copy of the Bible. He fell unconscious to the floor.

Celia laid the Bible on the floor next to him and checked his pulse—it was strong and steady.

Quickly Celia ran to the phone and called 911. "Someone hit Father Stubblefield! He's in his office at Saint Bartholomew's," she said over the concerned operator's questions and immediately hung up.

Celia dashed to the door and grabbed two candles and a book of matches from a hallway alcove. "Sorry, Father," she muttered as she raced to the small door behind the altar. "If it makes ya feel any better, I'm probably going to hell anyway"

* * * * *

Freitas stared at the wooden bridge. "I am so sick of this shit," she groused.

Flanigan shone his flashlight over her head. "Doesn't look so bad," he said. "Assuming we have a key for that wonderful door on the other side."

"Maybe it's not locked," Freitas said with futility.

Parker tested the first plank with her foot. "Someone built all this shit? Carved out these chambers and set up these damn bridges and crap? I mean, is this someone's idea of a good time?"

"Vampires," Freitas said.

"Yeah." Flanigan snarked. "Because no human would build a bridge this way."

With difficulty, Parker stepped around Freitas and moved onto the bridge. She took a few test steps forward. "See? Just like the kids' park in midtown," she grinned.

Freitas muttered a curse under her breath and followed her with Flanigan bringing up the rear. The bridge barely swayed under their weight as they made their way toward the ornate carved wood door on the other side.

Suddenly, Parker vanished from sight with a wordless cry.

"Shit!" Freitas shouted, leaning over the side. The bridge swayed alarmingly beneath them and Flanigan braced himself on the rope handrail. "Parker, you okay?"

"No!" Parker shouted, her voice rising up from the shadows. "My ass hurts! You two okay?"

"Sure, we're peachy!" Flanigan called. "Of course, we didn't just fall a hundred feet into an abyss!"

Parker looked around. "Looks about fifteen to twenty!" she called ruefully. "Hey, there's a door down here."

Flanigan shone his flashlight around on the floor then onto Parker's smudged face. "You're dirty, girl," he grinned.

"Get that thing out of my face, you're killing my night vision," Parker returned.

Behind her, Parker heard a strange slipping sound. "Wait a second," she called, looking around.

Her flashlight pierced through the gloom.

"What? What's going on?" Freitas called.

"Oh shit," Parker breathed.

Quickly Parker scrambled away from the wall. "Don't jump down! Snake! There's a fucking snake down here!"

It slid out of the wall, at least twenty feet long, with a diamond-shaped head the size of a watermelon and scales a strange silvery-green color that Parker had never seen on a snake before. It seemed to sense exactly where she was and wound itself in an S pattern toward her.

"Shit! Shit!" Parker gasped, dropping her flashlight as she fumbled for her service pistol. The flashlight clattered to the ground and spun, its light flashing about in strange patterns. The snake moved in and out of the light, and Parker couldn't tell where it was.

Up on the bridge, Flanigan shone both his and Freitas' flashlights over the side, searching for the snake as Freitas aimed her sidearm over the side. She caught a glimpse of Parker's red hair in the shadows. "Parker, move!"

Abaddon

"That's the plan!" Parker shouted, dodging away from the light.

Freitas searched through the shadows, following Flanigan's light. For a moment, the beams flashed on Parker again and Freitas almost pulled the trigger in reflex.

"Shit!" she shouted. "Parker, look out! I don't wanna shoot you!"

"I don't want you to shoot me either!" Parker returned.

The snake darted into the light and Parker dashed to the left. Freitas' shot screeched along the stone.

It danced after her and now Parker could see it in the dim glow cast by her discarded flashlight, now out of reach. Its eyes caught hers for a second, dead and unblinking.

Parker thumbed off the safety and fired.

Lightning-fast, the snake's head darted forward. Her bullet missed, striking the stone wall on the far side. Its fang clamped onto Parker's leg in a huge quicksilver pain that screamed up into her body. Parker jerked backward but the snake was clamped on to her calf.

"Fuck!" Parker cried, aiming for farther down the body of the snake. She shot it again, a small hole appearing in its body. Black ichor poured out of the hole and its body shuddered. It released her for a second, rearing back to bite her again.

Suddenly Flanigan leapt down, landing on the snake's back with a heavy grunt. The snake shot its head around toward him as Parker struggled to aim. He rode it like a bronco, holding tight to the snake as it writhed beneath him.

Freitas shot from above, exploding the snake's head in a mass of tangled, blackened flesh.

"Motherfuck," Parker said, stumbling against the wall.

"Let me look at that," Flanigan said, stepping over the snake's body to kneel in front of Parker.

"Look at you, all brave and shit," Parker said heavily, sliding down the stone wall to a sitting position.

"You inspired me," Flanigan said, frowning at her leg.

Above them, Freitas jumped down in an ungainly leap, losing her balance and falling over for a moment before scrambling to them.

"Sorry about this." Flanigan grabbed the fabric of her pants and ripped them open, exposing the bloodied flesh of her calf.

"S'okay, it wasn't one of my favorites," Parker managed.

Freitas knelt beside her, staring at the bloody hole in Parker's leg. "Shit, do you think that thing was poisonous?"

"Never saw anything like it before," Flanigan said, cracking open the first-aid kit. "Now aren't you glad I brought this?"

He pressed a small plunger-like device against the bloody hole in Parker's leg and pulled back on it. Parker let out a grunt of pain as the plunger filled with a thin, bloody liquid.

"Shit, what the fuck is that stuff?" Freitas muttered.

"Ow," Parker managed.

Flanigan emptied the plunger onto the ground, repeated the process and more liquid came out of the hole. He kept going, moving faster as he tried to suck the venom out of her leg.

Parker bit her lip hard and suddenly there was someone holding her hand. She grabbed hold and looked over at her partner, kneeling beside her with an unreadable look in her eyes.

"It's bleeding freely now," Flanigan said at last, pressing a thick square of gauze over the wound. "There's likely some in your bloodstream."

"Really," Parker said, aiming for sarcasm but failing. She felt very faint and light, as though she might float away.

Flanigan was checking the pulse at her throat, his hazel eyes clouded with concern as he shone the flashlight in her eyes, watching her pupils. "We've got to get her out of here,

Detective," he said to Freitas. "I don't know how bad that stuff is but it's definitely—"

"Hey," Parker said weakly. "Do you hear something?"

* * * * *

Samantha, Ryan and Drew stepped out of the last tunnel. They stood together beneath a stone archway carved with the word ABADDON, their scimitars in hand, but none of them moved.

The vast stone chamber was filled with endless steps and platforms, disappearing into unseen passageways and connecting with each other in a pattern that made no sense. Lit by flickering torches along the wall, the shadows played havoc, reaching up to the ceiling, lost in darkness.

And everywhere there were vampires.

Some were curled up on platforms, sleeping like kittens in a pile. Others lounged on stairs, staring indolently at the three newcomers. Most wore cloaks, each the same, though they wore different things underneath—one a simple T-shirt and jeans, another a slinky black vinyl jumpsuit. About six of them stood together on the left, armed with swords not much different than the scimitars they carried. Still others simply milled about, unheeding of the newcomers.

The sense of power in the room was overwhelming. It struck Samantha like an unseen wave, buffeting her inside her mind. She stumbled a little and her headache flared more brightly.

"Diego?" Ryan whispered.

Samantha shook her head, making the pain swell. "These are still individuals. They haven't lost themselves in their master like Diego's kiss did. But they're definitely a kiss, bound to a master."

"They're ignoring us," Ryan murmured.

Samantha tilted her head. "Let's fix that."

She stepped forward past the arch and the guard immediately reacted by standing at attention and advancing toward her.

"Zorathenne!" Samantha shouted at the top of her lungs.

Everyone stopped. Then all the vampires immediately retreated to the platforms, crouching above their heads or cringing into the shadows. The guards dispersed behind them, blocking their way back. That was fine by Samantha, whose head was filled with roaring pain that seemed to block out anything else. At this point, she hoped someone would kill her soon, to end this agony inside her head.

From the passageway on the far side, a lovely woman appeared, moving in elegant grace. Her skin was the dark color of rich chocolate and smooth as velvet, her voluptuous body wrapped in flaming-red silk that flowed about her limbs but was bound tightly over her torso. It left her shoulders bare in the glimmering light. Her head was elegantly bald, as though no hair had ever grown there and none ever would. She had the exotic beauty of an Egyptian carving and a single earring dangling from her right ear was her only decoration.

She stepped out onto the largest platform, which stood like a dais at the far end of the chamber.

Samantha, Ryan and Drew strode forward with a confidence that Samantha at least did not feel. This was what they had come to do—to challenge this woman and her minions. She had not expected the aura of power coming off this woman, flowing like bands of energy through to the vampires crouched all around them.

Samantha was going to her death and she knew it, welcomed it. But she would know why Danny had died before she went to join him.

"Welcome," Zorathenne said, her husky voice made into something warm and liquid, flowing over them. It was hard to resist that warmth, comforting and maternal. Samantha felt a nearly irresistible urge to go to her, as though Zorathenne's embrace would make the pain stop, the blessed ease cooling her fevered brow. But through the power, she could feel Zorathenne's intent—she wanted them, wanted them all under her control, and she would seduce them in whatever way she could—terror or love. Zorathenne knew them all, knew their names and their intent.

She had been waiting for them.

Samantha opened her mouth to speak the challenge, remembering Cristoval's brief teachings all those years ago. But she never got the words past her throat.

Drew lunged forward with his scimitar, shouting something incoherent as he swung the sword toward Zorathenne.

"Drew, no!" Ryan shouted. "The challenge!"

Zorathenne never moved. A young-looking vampire crouching nearby instantly leaped in front of her. Drew's scimitar penetrated deep into the young man's shoulder, sinking down into his chest. Horrified, Drew pulled it back. The vampire sank to his knees, coughing great gouts of blood onto the floor.

Drew raised his scimitar again and immediately a mass of vampires swelled in front of him, interposing their bodies to protect her. Drew tried to push past them without hurting them but they surrounded him in a mass of grasping hands and flailing limbs. They pulled the scimitar from his hands and dragged him forward before Zorathenne.

"No!" Samantha cried, but more vampires had appeared to restrain her and Ryan. She struggled against their hands but there were too many of them.

Zorathenne stepped forward toward Drew, who was held kneeling before her.

"Sweet Andrew," she murmured, sliding a hand alongside his face. "You should have challenged me. You might have had a chance."

Drew glared upward, his staid face contorted with hate. Samantha could hardly recognize him. "I know you killed her," he spat. "I gave you my answer months ago, and you killed her out of spite. You deserve no warning, no mercy."

Zorathenne smiled, revealing sharp white fangs that contrasted with her lovely dark skin. "But you will receive my...mercy," she whispered, and lowered her face to his.

Drew tried to turn away. But the vampires forced his head back before her.

"Oh Christ," Ryan cried, throwing himself against the restraining arms of the vampires holding them.

Zorathenne kissed Drew, deep and strong, as her vampires held him still and unwilling. It went on for at least a minute as Samantha felt Zorathenne's power surging over Drew and enveloping him. It was almost visual, a curtain of power flowing from her and nearly obscuring him from Samantha's senses.

Zorathenne released him with her mouth first, staring into his eyes and holding him in her power. Drew's eyes widened and his mouth opened in a silent scream.

Zorathenne stepped back. Without so much as a word from her, the vampires released Drew and faded back to the platforms. Drew sagged to the floor and Zorathenne retreated to her dais, calm in her triumph.

The hands holding Samantha and Ryan finally released. They ran to Drew and Samantha turned him over. Drew stared at the shadowed ceiling, horror in his eyes as tears streamed down his face. Samantha reached out to his mind and was met with the impenetrable wall of Zorathenne's power. She had enfolded Drew into her kiss and bound him to her will. Whatever silent shadows played in his mind, Zorathenne controlled them.

"For nothing, it was all for nothing," Drew whispered.

"Not yet," Ryan insisted, gripping Drew's hand. "There's still two of us. When she's dead, you'll be free."

Drew shook his head in misery. "You don't understand," he whispered. "She didn't...it wasn't..."

His words cut off as Zorathenne laughed from above them, her high, sweet laughter echoing around the room like the bright tinkle of a wind chime.

Samantha raised horrified eyes to Ryan. "We were wrong," she whispered.

Ryan's eyes were as haunted as hers. "Diego played us."

"She didn't kill them," Samantha said.

"Of course not," slid a new voice, silky and cajoling.

Samantha stood up and turned to face Zorathenne.

Cristoval stood beside her. In his hand, he held up Isabel's claddagh ring.

Chapter Seven

Parker was very pale and getting paler by the minute—at least as far as Freitas could tell in the thin light. Parker's heartbeat was racing fast and breathing seemed to be growing more difficult for her as she lay on the cold stone.

Both Flanigan and Freitas had tried to climb back up onto the bridge. Then Flanigan tried to lift Freitas up so she could grab the bridge. Neither approach worked. The bridge was just out of their reach, even when they tried to stand on the dead body of the snake.

"Goddammit!" Freitas shouted after a third attempt to scale the walls. She paced the room in frustration.

Flanigan was checking Parker's vital signs again. "Stay with me, Parker," he said.

"Not going...anywhere," Parker breathed, smiling.

Flanigan peered into her eyes again. "You better not. I'd definitely miss you."

There was a sound from above and Freitas pulled her gun. "Shit! Who's there?"

Celia's face peeked over the side. Her spiky black hair was dripping wet.

"Goddamn, am I glad to see you!" Freitas shouted. "Parker's hurt, I need you to—"

In a second, Celia had jumped to the floor, as Freitas and Flanigan both shouted, "NO!" at the top of their lungs. Parker couldn't help laughing weakly.

"Goddammit, Celia, we needed someone up top!" Freitas fumed, putting away her gun.

Celia ran over to Parker and knelt beside her, looking at the bloody mess of her leg. "Don't look so bad," she said, nonchalant.

"Nothing but a scratch," Parker breathed. "I'm gonna remember…you disobeyed again…"

"Ground me," Celia retorted, staring at her.

Flanigan looked over at Celia. "I don't think you're any taller than Freitas," he said ruefully. "But I can try lifting you back onto the bridge."

"To do what?" Celia snapped.

"Go for help, numbskull!" Freitas shouted. "Now no one knows we're here, unless the priest thinks to call them!"

"He'll tell 'em when he wakes up," Celia said absently, looking at Parker.

"Bad," Parker whispered. "You're definitely grounded." Celia almost smiled.

Freitas leaned over Parker, her face somber. "I need your gun, kid," she said softly.

"Not dead yet," Parker whispered back, smiling at her partner.

"Smart-ass," Freitas said, gently taking the pistol from Parker's holster. "I'll be giving this right back to you."

Flanigan stared at Freitas. "You are not going through that door alone."

"Damn skippy," Freitas said. "They sicced the goddamn snake on her, they might know how to save her. Or at least another way back up top."

"Or they'll have you for a snack," Flanigan returned. "I should go with you."

"C'mon, Flanigan, you ever swung a punch in your life? What kind of backup will you be?" Freitas retorted. "Besides, you're the only paramedic in this chamber, last I looked. You need to stay with Parker."

"I can back you up," Celia offered.

"NO," Freitas and Parker chorused.

Flanigan shook his head. "This is a bad idea, not to mention you're taking both our weapons," he said.

"Got to," Freitas said, squeezing Parker's hand again. "You just hold on, kid. I'll be right back."

"Annie, don't be an idiot," Parker whispered, her breath faint.

Freitas smoothed Parker's hair back from her head. "Can't help it, kid," she said softly as she checked the gun clip. "I learned it from you."

Freitas stepped out of the short tunnel into the weirdest room she'd ever seen. It was as though all the staircases in town had been removed to this room, leading to randomly placed platforms and doorways throughout the enormous chamber.

The instant she stepped into the room, there were a hundred eyes on her. Vampires, crouching on platforms and staircases, and each of them glaring at her with a baleful eye. A few hissed at her and Freitas thumbed the safety off both guns.

Brilliant, because you'll be able to slow down about twenty to forty of them and the other sixty can eat you at their leisure, Freitas thought. *Flanigan was right and Parker's going to taunt you about this in the afterlife.*

Vampire guards—so noted by their weapons, rather formidable-looking swords—immediately surrounded Freitas, who leveled her guns at them.

A second later, a stunning black woman clothed in red was suddenly there among the guards and they dispersed like smoke. "Human," the woman spat, sweeping around Freitas unnaturally fast. "You dare defile this place?"

"It wasn't easy to defile, believe me," Freitas snapped.

The woman hissed at Freitas, her face twisted in fury and madness, and it took all the self-control Freitas had not to start firing. Vampire or not, this woman was not all there. Past the trappings and the fancy language, there was crazy dancing in her eyes and Freitas knew crazy. But maybe she could still talk her way out of here.

The woman smiled, revealing those razor-sharp teeth, and Freitas started rethinking the "talk" idea. She tried to keep her eyes away from the woman's, to avoid being caught by her gaze.

"Human," the woman hissed, very close now.

"Wait! She's a cop, don't hurt her, she's a cop!" Lucas appeared beside the woman. "A police officer. If she goes missing, they'll come looking for us."

The woman glared at him and Lucas immediately knelt in supplication. "Forgive my insolence, Lady Zorathenne," he groveled.

Freitas had managed to fumble out her shield. "It's true, I'm a cop and there are other cops on the way," she said. "I'm here for help."

Zorathenne smiled. Then she laughed, a bright, insane laugh echoed almost mindlessly by the hordes around her. "Help!" she declared to the room. "The humans...want my help!" A low murmur of laughter rose from the vampires perched about the room, echoing in waves of madness.

"There's another human dying of a bite from that little leather pet you have." Freitas kept her eyes on Zorathenne. "This whole catacomb will be crawling with icky, disgusting humans pretty soon. They'll send the Chain Gang and it won't go so well for you."

"Or for you," Zorathenne returned, smiling.

Freitas grinned humorlessly, pretending she didn't think this group would eat the Chain Gang for lunch and still have room for supper. "Help for my friend. Help us get out of here. Then no one needs to find your little clubhouse down here."

Zorathenne grinned again. Suddenly about nine vampires moved toward the entranceway without Zorathenne speaking a word.

"Wait! No!" Freitas shouted, surging toward them.

Instantly Lucas was in front of her, blocking her path. "Move it, kid," Freitas snapped.

"I can't," Lucas whispered, tears brimming in his eyes. "She won't let me."

Freitas raised her gun and leveled it at Lucas' heart. "Move. Now."

"Lucas!" Celia shouted from the doorway where two vampires were dragging her by her arms. It took four of them to manhandle Flanigan in and an unconscious Parker was carried by three more.

Zorathenne swept past them to Parker, gazing down at her. "She's not gone yet," she said. "Take them to the cells."

The vampires converged on them. Freitas started shooting but after three fell, the fourth grasped her wrists with unholy strength and wrested both guns away from her. Lucas pocketed them and they half carried, half shoved the humans away into one of the passages with Zorathenne's laughter trailing after them.

Yup. This was definitely a bad idea, Freitas thought as the darkness swallowed them.

* * * * *

Samantha leaned against the dank stone wall, her eyes closed against the agony behind her eyes. Ryan was testing the stones in the walls, muttering to himself. She heard her own name and opened her eyes with difficulty. "Yes?"

"You have the quintessential bad ex problem, Samantha," Ryan grumbled. "I thought Cristoval was dead."

"Me too. Fiona said he was dead," Samantha murmured then uttered a bitter laugh. "Then again, she said that about

Diego. I suppose I really ought to stop taking Fiona's word in place of a death certificate."

There was a commotion in the hallway and the door flung open. Suddenly Flanigan, Freitas and Celia were shoved inside. A few vampires lay Parker's body down beside them. Then they faded out, leaving only Lucas.

"Oh my God," Ryan said, dropping beside Parker. Flanigan knelt beside her, taking her pulse. "Is she alive?"

"For now," Flanigan said, frowning.

Lucas stepped forward timidly. "The Lady Zorathenne will send a healer soon," he said. "She will not want a police officer to die down here. It would be...bad for us."

Celia rose to her feet, fury in her eyes. Lucas dropped his eyes, looking even paler.

"I had no choice," he said quietly.

Celia decked him, a hard and fast punch that threw him against the wall. Ryan and Freitas restrained her from a second punch with difficulty. Instead, she spat at him. "Fuck. You."

Samantha ignored them, kneeling beside Parker. She let down the barriers she had tried to keep up since coming here, reaching out to Parker's mind.

Closing her eyes, she saw the white void in which Parker floated, making up dreams as she went along. She saw a silvery-green snake dancing around the periphery as Parker stood watching Celia sleep, worry creasing her brow. She saw Diego's mad face for an instant. Then a girl she didn't know cowering in a filthy kitchen littered with spilled cocaine and tequila bottles.

"My sister," Parker whispered to her. "I let her go. I let her go and I never saw her again."

"Stay with us," Samantha murmured.

Parker turned to her, her fiery red hair muted in the white void. "I let her go."

Diego suddenly danced into view and Parker flinched. He fell on a body lying at their feet, feeding ravenously as the man screamed in a boy's voice.

Samantha cried out. "This isn't possible," she gasped. "This isn't your memory."

Diego looked up, his twisted face covered with Todd's blood. Todd lay still now, his policeman's uniform soaked with blood still pumping from the ripped hole in the center of his chest.

"Yours?" Parker asked, moving forward. "This was yours?"

Tears brimmed in Samantha's eyes. "He loved me," she whispered. "He loved me and he wanted to take me away. But Cristoval found out and he let Diego kill him in front of me."

"When he bit me, Diego showed me this moment and a few others, but this one, over and over," Parker said quietly. "I guess he thought, being a cop... He wanted me to know what he did to cops."

Samantha stepped forward, past Parker, and Diego vanished from view. Only Todd's body remained, his face frozen in final agony. She knelt beside him. "I saved his badge. It's under the carpet in my trunk. He was so proud of being a police officer, it was everything he was."

"Am I dying?" Parker asked.

Samantha looked up. "I hope not," she said quietly. "Please, don't go yet. Celia needs you."

"Celia doesn't need anyone," Parker said bitterly.

"Yes, she does," Samantha said. "She doesn't show it. But she needs you."

"Samantha!" Ryan's voice jolted Samantha out of the void, away from Parker and back into the cell. "Are you all right?"

"Yes," she said hesitantly. "So is Kelly, but not for long."

Ryan's face was concerned, hovering in the flickering light. As Samantha looked around, she saw two more vampires had arrived to stand with Lucas.

"I am a healer," one of them said, stepping forward.

Freitas and Ryan both stood between him and Parker.

"Trust me, he can help," Lucas said.

"Trust you, sure," Freitas snapped. Lucas dropped his gaze.

No one moved for a minute. Then Celia spoke. "Let him try."

Freitas looked over at Celia, and after a long moment, she stepped aside, Ryan beside her. He put a comforting hand on her shoulder and for once Celia did not flinch away from touch.

The healer knelt beside Parker. He shook some herbs out of a small leather pouch and pressed them against Parker's leg. Then he leaned over her, lowering his face to her neck.

"Hold it," Freitas snapped, and her hand instantly flew to her empty holster.

"It's how it's done," Samantha murmured then looked up at Freitas. "Trust *me*."

The healer struck, feeding from Parker's neck. He drank for only a moment, barely tasting her. Then he got back to his feet.

"She will live," he said, and left with the other one, who had not spoken. After a moment, Lucas followed them, letting the cell door clang shut.

Flanigan checked Parker's vital signs again. "Her pulse is slower but she's not waking up any time soon," he said. "Voodoo bullshit."

Samantha leaned against the wall, weary. "To a native tribesman of ancient times, a CAT scan would seem like magic," she said. "Vampire healers are very rare, but they work. I'm surprised Zorathenne has one."

The door swung open again and Cristoval stalked in.

He was as darkly handsome as he had been the first night she met him on the Baltimore pier, Samantha thought. She had been a naïve young girl, lost on an ill-advised excursion into the city, and he had been a mysterious foreigner who charmed her with his kindness and courtly deference. His hair still shone with the same black luster, his smile as charming as ever. There he stood before her, in real flesh and blood, and she was half tempted to ask the others if they could see him as well. Was she imagining him, imagining his appearance beside Zorathenne? Had she finally gone mad?

Samantha felt his power trying to wash over her, rolling against her defenses like gentle waves rebuffed by the rocks of the shore. His power was muted now, shared with Zorathenne. She fended him off with difficulty, her headache a thousand times worse in a paralyzing heartbeat against her eyes and temples.

"My beloved Miranda," he said, bowing before her. "It has been far too long."

Samantha resisted the urge to tell him her name was not Miranda and never had been. Instead, she remained silent.

Freitas stepped away from Cristoval, her hand still instinctively going to her empty holster. She circled him quietly, trying to stay out of his peripheral vision as she moved behind him.

In a second, Cristoval had snapped around and caught Freitas by the throat, holding her up against the wall. Ryan tried in vain to pull him off as Celia and Flanigan leaped toward him.

"Stop it!" Samantha shouted.

Cristoval's eyes narrowed as he smiled, teeth gleaming.

"Back down, everyone," Samantha commanded. Ryan stepped away and Cristoval released Freitas. She stumbled over to Celia, coughing.

Cristoval extended a hand to Samantha. "Come for a walk, my dear," he said.

"Not happening," Ryan growled.

"Yes it is," Samantha said immediately as Cristoval's smile grew wider. She could still read him perfectly, still sense his every mood and whim as though no time at all had passed since she last shared his bed. He would not hesitate to kill any of them and he would not make it quick or easy, and he would delight in the pain he caused. Even after all these decades, she still found herself trying to stand between his madness and human beings.

"Samantha," Ryan protested, and she turned to him.

"Trust me," she whispered, and he subsided.

Samantha stepped out of the cell with Cristoval. He extended an arm, which she pointedly ignored. It felt petty but she could not be such a hypocrite as to touch him. He was a walking nightmare, the past come to life, and she would walk with him, talk with him, but she would not touch him. It was perhaps fate that she would die at his hand—she had often thought she was cheating death for every hour since the night he made her into a vampire and she had always been meant to die under his mad, gleeful gaze.

But she would not touch him.

They walked through a seemingly endless maze of tunnels, silent at first. Then he began to point things out to her—here was the armory where they stockpiled weapons. Here was the workshop where they made the things they needed. The one thing he did not show her was a way out, and near as she could tell, there was nowhere to go.

"You've been busy," she said finally.

"I have had many years to find something to occupy myself," Cristoval replied, opening a door and stepping aside to allow Samantha to enter first.

It was a bedroom, gloriously appointed with a heavy wooden four-poster bed draped in red silk draperies and a mountain of red linens. Zorathenne lounged on the bed, catlike in her grace and smiling in welcome.

Samantha turned to face Cristoval as he entered behind her. "They came for Diego the night you died or so Fiona said," she said. "Did you escape with him? Or did he get the better of you?"

Cristoval's smile faltered and she could see the fury in him. Only for the first time, his anger held no terror for her. Once she would have fallen to her knees, immediately contrite. But her will was her own now and she was stronger.

Stronger than Cristoval. She tested the thought and found she liked it. It brought a humorless smile to her own face.

"Diego will be dealt with in time," Cristoval said stiffly.

Samantha laughed again, flopping into a chair swathed in decadent silk. "You couldn't handle him when you were his *master*," she needled him. "Now he has his own kiss, running around the world wreaking his madness... How could you, the consort to a vampire greater than yourself, ever hope to match him now?"

Cristoval's fury blazed from his eyes and Samantha felt a surge of triumph. Not from herself—from Zorathenne. Zorathenne was happy to see Cristoval tormented. There was real anger coming from the master vampire lounging on the bed, her seeming indolence belied by the fury Samantha sensed.

Samantha turned to Zorathenne. "You didn't know," she said calmly. "It was all him. He was conducting his own private war behind your back."

Zorathenne's easy smile didn't waver but there was a bit of pique in her eyes. "Your skills are as strong as I've been told," she smoothed with her velvet voice. Samantha's headache worsened and she felt that tug again, the unspoken promise that if she would go to Zorathenne, the pain would stop. All pain, the pain in her head and in her heart.

Come to me, child, and let me make you whole again, Zorathenne's voice cajoled in her mind. *Then I will not have to kill your pet humans.*

* * * * *

"One...two...three!" Ryan and Flanigan ran full-tilt at the door. It barely moved under the impact.

"Told ya," Celia said, still crouched by Parker's unconscious form.

"Relax, kiddo," Freitas said, sitting beside her. "Parker's a tough kid. She'll be okay."

"Yeah," Celia said, carefully moving a strand of hair off Parker's face.

Flanigan flopped on the floor. "I'm confused as hell," he said. "Is anyone going to explain what the flying fuck is going on?"

"If we get out of here, we'll give it a shot," Freitas said. "All you need to know right now is that we're in deep shit and I think we have no friends, and by the way, where the fuck is Sanford?"

Ryan's eyes dropped.

"Aw shit, he's not dead?" Freitas asked.

Ryan shook his head. "Worse. He attacked her without a challenge. She was not bound by the rules and so she was able to take him into her kiss."

Flanigan raised his hand. "Help. I need some definitions."

"A kiss is sort of a telepathic link among vampires," Freitas said. "They're all under one vampire's control, and my guess is it's Zorathenne. She can make them do anything she wants. But you can break out of a kiss, right? Samantha did it."

Ryan looked miserable. "She's the only one I ever knew who did," he said. "She's a power that I've never seen, that no one ever has. Her mental ability is the equivalent of a massive locomotive, idling at the station. Cristoval couldn't hold her and she escaped."

"That's good for us, right? To have someone that powerful on our side?" Flanigan asked.

"Not so much," Freitas said.

Her eyes met Ryan's.

"What? What are you talkin' about?" Celia asked.

"If Zorathenne takes Samantha into her fold, we are deeply screwed," Ryan said.

"Not just us," Freitas said. "With Samantha in her kiss, I doubt Zorathenne will be content to sit down here in her Batcave."

Flanigan closed his eyes. "Christ. You're talking about war. A street war."

"We'd win though," Celia offered. "I mean, we got guns and shit. The Army. We'd win."

Freitas looked over at her. "We got guns that don't kill them and they can freeze us just by looking at us, not to mention the fact that we're their food and they've had centuries to plan," she said. "And we've got tens of thousands of vampires up top who are tired of being treated like shit. If you were them, which side would you take?"

Ryan got up and kicked at the door again. "We've got to get out of here," he said.

* * * * *

Zorathenne touched Samantha's face gently as she stepped out from behind the screen. She was swathed in ice-blue silk, similar to Zorathenne's red garments. Her hair was loose, tumbling in corn-silk waves about her shoulders.

"You are lovely, my dear," Zorathenne cooed, moving over beside her. "But your face! You need a cool cloth for your eyes."

"My head hurts," Samantha said dully.

"Crockett!" Cristoval called. He was lounging on a chaise nearby. A male vampire stumbled into view from one of the passages on the right. His face was twisted and burned into a permanent sneer, most of his hair burned off. He wore rags, his arms and legs marked with scorched burns. There were two fingers missing from his left hand.

"Good God," Samantha breathed, and turned to Zorathenne. "This is how you treat your kiss?"

Zorathenne's cool demeanor vanished and suddenly her black eyes were filled with cold, glittering fury. "This *thing* is no part of me," she spat. "In his *human* life, he led the mob that came to the church, when the Inferno came. He defiled a holy place. He struck a priest and dragged a man from sanctuary to burn him alive on holy ground."

Samantha stared at Crockett, whose eyes seemed dull and blank as he cringed before her. "You made him a vampire? And tortured him?"

"Torture is a subjective term," Zorathenne said smoothly. "I did nothing to him that the humans did not do to us."

Samantha reached out a hand toward Crockett. "The Chain Gang," she murmured. "Silver chains and sunlight."

"Every day for a hundred years, in a chamber where the sun can shine," Zorathenne replied, her power growing like a living thing against Samantha's skin as her emotions rose again. "I have no knowledge of a hell or a heaven, my dear. Killing him would have been far too merciful. Instead I create the hell I wished for him. He lives in it daily, and if he serves me well, I shall take no more parts of him away."

Samantha stared at the stumps of the two missing fingers, which Crocket immediately tried to hide.

"He was your...consort? The man Crockett burned?" Samantha asked.

Zorathenne paused. "He was," she said, her voice quieter for a moment. "A gentle and kind man, a husband in every way. They took him from me. So you see, we have much in common, my dear. We both have lost something precious, something special, but we can make a better life for ourselves."

For an instant Samantha let herself think of Danny and she lost her breath. "There's nothing left," she whispered.

"The humans are a pestilence, a vicious plague on the earth that rightly belongs to us," Zorathenne said, her voice growing in power and intensity. "This is our city, our earth, and they have done nothing with it in all these centuries but destroy and torment. This is *my* city now, under my thrall. The vampires of power belong to me, just as Andrew now belongs me. He resisted me but none can resist me forever."

Samantha stared at her. "You're mad," she whispered.

Zorathenne leaned toward her, her voice almost motherly in its calm tone. "Do not weep for the humans, my child," she cajoled, the gentleness of her tone in direct contrast to the insanity of her words. "It is their hatred that has brought this upon them. They could have left us alone, to live among them in peace. But they come with their torches and their ignorance, they round us up and torture us with their petty devices, they burn us before their altars as less-than-human sacrifices to their God. We are more than human, more than they can dream, and the earth by rights shall pass to those who have suffered."

Her voice softened further. "I know you will not weep for them, my child. Did you not declare, this very night, to 'let them burn'?"

Samantha gaped at her. "Fiona too?" she whispered.

Cristoval stepped in, smiling. "Not Fiona, alas—not yet," he amended. "Dear Brent, so devoted to her. He was easy to convince."

"The hell you say," Samantha shot back, and Cristoval's smile faded. "Brent would never betray Fiona in a thousand years."

"How little you understand the heart," Zorathenne said, smiling. "You do not motivate someone by making them fear you. You bring them to your side by threatening that which they love. He would die for Fiona, but he would do worse than that if he thinks he will save her life."

Samantha's eyes glittered. "You bitch," she spat.

Zorathenne laughed. "Sticks and stones, child," she said. "Do not tell me you do not crave power. I know what you did to little Diego."

Samantha shook her head. "Little Diego. You don't know him or you would never dismiss him so easily."

"Diego is a whelp, no threat," Cristoval said, but she knew he was lying.

Samantha turned to Cristoval, suddenly furious. "You let him go," she spat. "You let Diego go. You let him run rampant, let him kill, let him enslave vampires to the point where they no longer have minds or souls of their own... You *let* it happen. All the bloodshed, the humans' hate as they search the world for Diego, it is all because of you."

"Diego is not my concern," Cristoval said shortly, all trace of courtly gentility gone. "You are. Zorathenne wishes you to join our kiss."

Samantha stood frozen for a moment.

Zorathenne swept around her. "Think of it, child," she said. "Stand with me and Cristoval. Meld our power together. Imagine the things we could do together. The greatest kiss the vampire world has ever known." She traced a finger up Samantha's bare arm.

Samantha laughed. "And you thought killing my...killing people would be a good recruitment tactic?"

Cristoval smiled but his smile was full of menace. He took a bow. "You are here, aren't you?"

Zorathenne looked at Cristoval and he immediately fell silent. "If you think we lack a certain...compassion...then you could provide that," she said. "Perhaps we will need your voice to deal fairly with the humans."

"You're lying," Samantha spat. "I remember the kiss. I remember how Cristoval used it to control us, force us to allow atrocities, kept us silent when Diego's madness threatened all of us."

Cristoval's smile never faltered and she could sense from him a memory he wanted her to share, a powerful moment from the days when she still loved him. In a moment, she could feel his hands on her skin, his breath on her neck, her own cries of passion in his arms. It swept over her with power, heat and sex and the rush within her body as she lay with him in the summer twilight. He wanted to remind her how good it had been, those few years before it became dark, twisted and evil. Before Diego. He stirred the shadowy sexual heat within her that she kept locked away in fear.

She steeled herself against the memory with the repeating thought—*Another time. Another life. Another time. Another life.*

"And is this life so much more appealing?" Cristoval grinned. "A lovely white picket fence with a pet human who can never truly comprehend the darkness in you?"

"In you, not in me," Samantha protested.

Zorathenne stepped over to whisper in her ear. "You are a predator, child," she whispered. "Do not deny what you are. Be with us and embrace what you truly are." She touched Samantha's arm again, lightly. "I would let you keep your pet humans, my dear. I am generous with those who belong to me."

* * * * *

Parker coughed a little and immediately Celia and Freitas were at her side. Parker's eyes opened slowly, blinking in the dim light.

"Hey, kid," Freitas said, a ghost of a smile on her face.

"I'm not dead," Parker whispered.

Freitas grinned. "See, it's that astute observational skill that makes you such a good cop," she said.

Parker's eyes flicked over to Celia. "Are we screwed?"

"Gettin' there," Celia replied. "I'm glad you're not dead."

Parker started to laugh but lost her breath and was quiet for a second.

Flanigan leaned over her, checking her pulse again. "Welcome back," he said, grinning.

Parker struggled to sit up and Flanigan pushed her back down gently. "That's enough," he said. "No marathons until we have somewhere to go."

The door clicked open and Freitas and Ryan were on their feet in a second. Lucas stepped in, carrying both guns and all three scimitars.

"There isn't much time," Lucas whispered. "You've got to hurry."

Freitas took the guns and a scimitar, and Ryan and Flanigan each took a scimitar. Celia glared at Lucas. "Thought ya couldn't help it," she accused.

"She's gonna catch me as soon as she's not distracted anymore," Lucas said. "You've got to move fast. As soon as she's done with Samantha, she'll have a feast."

"With us as the main course?" Flanigan asked.

Lucas nodded. "It's, uh, tradition."

"Bullshit," Ryan retorted. "None of this shit is tradition."

"The Lady Zorathenne makes up her own tradition and we follow it or we end up in the sunroom," Lucas said. "If that means we 'celebrate' by eating a few homeless and runaways, there's nothing we can do about it."

Celia glared at him and Lucas' eyes filled with misery. "I'm so sorry," he said. "I wanted to tell you."

"We don't have time for this!" Flanigan said. "Unless anyone here feels like being the main course at Zorathenne's big feast, let's get the hell out of here."

Ryan shook his head. "Not without Samantha."

"Samantha's gone, she's gonna join the kiss!" Lucas said.

"The hell you say," Ryan shot back. "Samantha would never join them."

"She doesn't have a choice!" Lucas said. "They'll trick her into thinking she's not really joining, just 'allying' or something. Or they'll blackmail her with your lives or they'll just play games with her head until she can't tell the difference between reality and their fantasies. Zorathenne and Cristoval, they got a thousand ways to fuck with your head and Samantha doesn't stand a chance. As soon as she gives in, it's all over, and if you're still here, you're only going to be the first ones to die! Zorathenne's got an entire army above and below, and the only way she can control them all through the new Inferno is with Samantha. If you get out, you can warn the humans, maybe give them a chance!"

Freitas lowered her head. "He's right, Ryan. We need way more reinforcements to deal with this."

"Fuck that," Ryan returned. "I came here with Samantha and I'm not leaving without her."

"As long as we're here, we're leverage," Freitas said. "Maybe without us to threaten, Samantha can resist."

"I second the 'not getting eaten' vote," Parker said weakly, sitting up against the wall.

"Fine, you get out and warn people and avoid the soirée, I'm going after Samantha," Ryan said.

"They'll kill you, Ryan," Freitas said quietly.

Ryan met her eyes and both fell quiet.

"No," Freitas insisted. "Isabel wouldn't want that."

"They killed her," Ryan said. "They killed her and I'm going to know why before I leave. And I'm taking Samantha with me. One way or the other."

"The hell?" Celia retorted.

Ryan looked at her. "If Samantha is what Zorathenne needs to start a vampire Inferno throughout the city, then Zorathenne can't have Samantha," he said woodenly. "I'll stop her if I can. And if I can't…"

"You cannot kill Samantha," Freitas snapped. "No. Fucking. Way."

"What do you suggest, *Detective*?" Ryan exploded. "This is a nightmare any way we turn! You think I want to kill my best friend? You think I wanted to be here in the first place? I didn't want any of this! I want it all to be over, and I want Drew to be free and I want Samantha safe at home with Danny and I want Isabel back goddammit, but there's no clean way out of this!"

Freitas stared at him as Lucas glanced out into the hallway in fear. "Fuck," she said. "Flanigan, you and Celia get Parker out of here. Lucas, show them the way. Ryan and me, we're going after Samantha."

"Wait," Parker said, raising a hand toward her.

Freitas knelt beside Parker. "You're in no shape to help, kid," she said, not unkindly. "They can get you home safe."

"Don't like sneaking out halfway through the game," Parker murmured, looking up at her partner in frustration.

Freitas looked at her for a long moment. "Snake or no snake, there's no one I'd rather fight with," she said softly, taking Parker's hand.

Parker grasped her hand tightly. "Get Samantha," she said quietly. "Next time, I'm taking point."

* * * * *

The sound was beginning to grow. The vampires were gathering in the main chamber, more than Samantha had ever realized could possibly be in this strange underground. They lined the stairways and platforms, crowded together, each clad in a dark cloak. Drew sat near the foot of the main dais, his eyes blank and staring. Samantha had tried to reach him with her mind but was rebuffed again by Zorathenne's power. He sat there in a hell of his own mind, utterly still.

Samantha stood beside Zorathenne, her ice blue silk contrasting to Zorathenne's vivid red and Cristoval's black cloak. The vampires gathered around them and she could feel their power growing throughout the room.

"Come to me now, my child," Zorathenne commanded. The vampires leaned forward, and Samantha could sense them, waiting under Zorathenne's control, but writhing and impatient.

Samantha stood before her but did not meet her eyes.

"I want to know something first," she said, and a murmur spread through the vampires, quickly quelled. They were not expecting this. "You approached Drew to convince him to join you. When he wouldn't, Cristoval killed his wife. But you never approached me before you killed Danny." She swallowed past the lump in her throat.

"I needed you to come here unencumbered," Cristoval said smoothly from her side.

Despite herself, Samantha's eyes filled with angry tears, looking at Zorathenne so she wouldn't have to look at him. "You hate me that much. You son of a bitch."

Cristoval bowed again. "Not a complete son of a bitch," he said. "After all, how could I resist the temptation to learn from the man who replaced me in your bed?"

Now Samantha turned to him, gaped at him. "What?" In her shock, she forgot not to look directly at him.

Cristoval's eyes filled hers, black and glittering with madness. "How's your headache, Samantha?"

In a sudden rush, the pain departed, leaving sweet pain-free bliss in her head. Samantha staggered to her knees as the unseen grip was released. It was as though a vise had been wrapped around her head, and with it gone, she could think again. Could sense...

"Danny?" she whispered.

Cristoval smiled.

On a platform in the far corner, Ryan could not suppress a gasp. He and Freitas were huddled beneath cloaks. "Danny's alive?" he whispered.

"Shit, forgot to mention that," Freitas muttered. "They didn't find his body in the community center. That's what Flanigan was trying to tell you guys when you gave him the slip at the club."

Ryan shuddered. "All this for nothing..."

"Not quite," Freitas said with grim resolve. "There's still Isabel." Ryan didn't speak. "No, Ryan, there's no chance for her. Isabel is dead."

"I know," Ryan said, his hand clenched on the flame-carved handle of his scimitar.

Crockett lunged out of a tunnel. Cristoval waved a hand, and the crowd of cloaked vampires to the right parted like an ocean. Crockett dragged Danny Carton out onto a lower platform. He was weak and pale, an ugly bruise to the side of his head and dried blood encrusted in his hair. The vampires held him still on the platform but he clearly was not fighting them.

"Danny!" Samantha cried, running across the chamber toward the platform. Relief and happiness washed over her like the tide that had smoothed the headache from her mind.

Cristoval had been blocking her sense of him, causing her pain as he hid Danny's mind from her. Danny was there, alive and whole and breathing, and she could sense his untouched mind through their link.

A crowd of vampires moved between them, holding her back as she struggled against them. Her hand fell to the scimitar at her side, the sword they had returned to her when she agreed to appear on the dais. "Danny!"

Danny looked up and his eyes met hers. In that instant, she could sense him again, that wonderful sense of *him* still a part of her, still making her whole. *Samantha, thank God*, he thought to her. *They said…they told me…*

I love you, Samantha thought to him in a sudden rush. *I love you, Daniel Robert Carton, and I'm so sorry I didn't tell you everything, I'll never—*

"That is enough," Zorathenne said, her voice cutting through the crowd like a sword. There was real anger in her tone and Samantha realized this too had been kept from her. Cristoval had set the fires, killed humans and hidden Danny in these catacombs, all behind her back. Zorathenne's anger was hot and strong, but it was leveled at Cristoval, not them.

Samantha turned to face her. "You're slipping, *Lady* Zorathenne," she said. "I do believe you're losing control of your kiss. All of them, they're starting to become their own persons again, aren't they? Too many for you to control?"

"Hardly, child," Zorathenne said, but there was little conviction in her voice.

Samantha advanced on Zorathenne, her own power building inside. It was like a wave she felt inside her, swelling and growing until she thought surely they must see it. Surely she must glow or something, suffused with light. "I'd wager it's only Cristoval boosting your power that's kept them under control this long," she said. "But the more you add, the weaker you become. There's no vampire ever made who can control the entire world, Zorathenne. Any attempt to do so is madness."

"We'll see," Zorathenne said smoothly. "With you joined to me, we'll see what can be accomplished."

"But what about Cristoval?" Samantha asked. "Does he get a demotion?"

Cristoval's face darkened and he stepped up beside Zorathenne almost defensively. Zorathenne did not look at him.

"Uh-oh, *beloved,*" Samantha taunted him. "I do believe you might be in trouble with your *mistress.*" She felt the hot surge of frustrated fury from Cristoval and smiled.

"Enough," Zorathenne commanded. "You will come now, Samantha, and kneel before me."

Samantha shook her head. "I don't think so," she said. "You can send your minions to hold me if you wish, but I think you'll find I'm a bit too much of a mouthful for even you to swallow without my consent. You know I can fight them — and I'll win."

"I know no such thing," Zorathenne returned. "But you will not fight."

"Oh? And why is that?" Samantha asked.

Zorathenne smiled but there was no humor in it. "Because if you do, I will bring your friends before you one by one and you will watch them die," she said calmly. "The humans will feed my kiss. I will drink the vampire myself. They will die at your feet."

"And I'm supposed to believe you'll let them go if I do what you want?" Samantha asked. "I may not be as old as you are, Zorathenne, but I am hardly a fool."

"Of course I will let them go," Zorathenne said. "A police officer, vanishing into my realm? That is trouble I do not want, at least not until we rise to reclaim our streets."

Samantha faltered a moment.

Don't do it, Danny said in her mind. *They wouldn't want that.*

"Of course that includes your pet," Zorathenne interjected. "He will hardly make a good meal, the condition he's in. But he will feed us well enough."

Samantha's mind screamed at that image—of Danny lying beneath the ravenous hunger of vampires. *Just like Todd, not again, I can't bear it again.*

Shh, I'm not Todd, Danny whispered in her mind.

But the others…

A step behind her and Samantha turned. Ryan strode past her, clad in a cloak. She suppressed a gasp.

"Your leverage is gone," Ryan told Cristoval and Zorathenne. "They're safe up above. You really are slipping."

Zorathenne's anger was scorching and huge, lashing out at the entire room. She did not speak, but it rolled through the room and even Samantha could feel it, buffeting her like a blast of hot wind. The vampires cringed as one and Samantha could not suppress a small smile. *Good on you, Annie,* she thought.

"We know why you killed Beth Sanford and why you came after Danny," Ryan said. "But I am no use to you. I do not have Drew's influence or Samantha's mental powers. Why Isabel?"

Neither answered him. Ryan looked from one impassive vampire to the other. "WHY?" he shouted.

"His hate," Samantha said, returning to stand beside Ryan. "Humans are the enemy, merely animals, isn't that right? We should not consort with animals?"

Cristoval bowed. "And you always would dally with them. I would have allowed you your human pets, Miranda, if only you had not tried to break with us. Was not the death of one enough?"

Samantha paused for a moment, staggering under the image Cristoval forced upon her—poor Todd, yet again, murdered in an alley. She tried to defend herself but Cristoval forced again with Zorathenne's power at least temporarily behind him. He forced her back to that alley, to Todd lying in a pool of blood, of Diego's bloodstained, smiling face. In the image, Todd kept becoming Danny, his face changing back and forth as she watched.

No, for the love of God not again, her mind cried. Somewhere Danny's mind was calling to her but Zorathenne and Cristoval kept interfering and she couldn't see anymore.

But Samantha pushed back and this time there was something behind her, some power other than hers. She did not recognize it, but she had no time to follow it back to its source.

"Not Danny," she said, her voice full of cold fury. "No more."

Cristoval shrugged. "Just another human," he said. "The pretty lady at your party…was that Isabel, Mr. Callahan? She tasted delicious. But so afraid…"

With a cry of fury, Ryan threw off his cloak and pulled his scimitar. "*Te Desafío!*" he shouted, just as Samantha had told him. She cried out in protest—it was a distraction, it was a way to stop her from fighting them, it was just what Cristoval wanted. Ryan ignored her, caught in his own maelstrom of fury and grief.

Samantha turned pleading eyes to Zorathenne but the ebony master shook her head. The rules of the *Desafío*, Samantha remembered, the rules Drew had broken and for which he had paid such a terrible price.

"*Accepto el Desafío,*" Cristoval said. He reached behind the dais and withdrew a sword. He stepped down into the center of the chamber, discarding his black cloak. Samantha had to retreat back toward a platform to the side.

Ryan and Cristoval circled each other for a moment, glaring in the flickering torchlight. Then Cristoval swung his sword, reaching farther than Ryan's slim scimitar. Ryan danced backward out of the way, dodging to the side as Cristoval swung another lightning-fast blow.

Cristoval was stronger, built heavy and muscled, but Ryan was lithe and fast. Their swords clanged together several times, dodging out of each other's way. Samantha met Danny's eyes over them, horrified. Suddenly the room seemed different, more dangerous and terrifying than any moment since arriving in this dark chamber. Before Danny had appeared, Samantha had felt as though she were fighting underwater, everything muted and slow and unimportant.

Now she had something to lose again. Danny's dear face stood out against the shadows and misery. She knew every line, every expression of his face. She needed no link to see his pain and she wanted nothing more than to fly to him, take him away from this ugliness and death, keep him safe from all of this misery and blood that she had worked so hard to escape.

I'm so sorry, her mind whispered to him, and he shook his head.

Ryan staggered backward under a renewed onslaught from Cristoval. Samantha tried to lend him strength but with no link between them, she could only watch helplessly. Cristoval was a trained fighter centuries before Ryan was born, and Ryan had been a peasant farmer before becoming a vampire.

Cristoval's sword clanged against Ryan's in a quickening pattern, striking again and again and again until a hard thrust struck it from Ryan's hand.

It skittered across the floor toward Samantha's feet.

Ryan dropped to his knees, his hands outstretched. He closed his eyes.

"I declare Cristoval the victor," Zorathenne crowed, her voice triumphant.

"No, dammit!" Danny cried.

Cristoval raised his sword and swung it downward.

Clang. Ryan's scimitar met Cristoval's sword just above Ryan's head. "*Te Desafío.*" Samantha held Ryan's scimitar firmly, the shock of the impact rocking to her shoulder and causing the blue silk of her garments to flutter about as though blown by wind.

"You cannot interfere," Cristoval said, glaring at her.

"I take up the challenge on Ryan Callahan's behalf," Samantha retorted. "*Te Desafío*, Cristoval."

Muttering rose in a wave throughout the vampires and Zorathenne raised a hand to quell it. Cristoval stepped back in confusion and looked to Zorathenne.

"A consort can challenge her master," Zorathenne said, smiling in triumph. "She can take up arms against her master if she believes it is in the best interest of her kiss."

"Samantha," Ryan pleaded. "Don't do this, please…this is why I came here."

Samantha dropped the scimitar and knelt beside Ryan, touching his face in sadness. "I know," she said. "But I told you once. I'm sorry, Ryan, but no."

"Don't do this to me," Ryan said brokenly.

Samantha shook her head. "I'm not doing it for you," she said softly. "I'm doing it for Isabel. This is what she would want. It's easy to die for someone, Ryan. It's much harder to live for them."

The vampires dragged Ryan away, hauling him up onto the platform beside Danny. Cristoval stepped back down to circle around Samantha, raising his sword.

"He's going to kill her, we have to stop this somehow," Danny whispered.

Ryan stared into the chamber. Samantha seemed different somehow, moving around the room with a feline grace. She drew her own scimitar, holding a sword in each hand. She suddenly seemed like the predator Cristoval had accused her of being, stalking him with a half smile on her face as though she were enjoying the moment.

Samantha's power grew around her. Even a vampire with Ryan's limited senses could tell that there were more than swords involved in this conflict.

"Miranda, you never could best me," Cristoval said, still circling. "In the best of times, you were not a match for me."

"My name is not Miranda," Samantha returned, raising one of the scimitars over her head. "And I no longer belong to you."

Samantha danced forward and stabbed at Cristoval, ripping through his sleeve. He jerked away, blood spreading on the torn fabric of his shirt.

Cristoval lunged forward and Samantha met him full force, their swords clanging together in a quickening beat. Cristoval swung his sword around and she ducked it, crouching low and kicking him hard in the stomach in a move Danny recognized from her training sessions with Sensei.

It was not the delicate dance of formal swordplay, one hand carefully tucked behind the back as they made noise with swords. It was a battle of power and will, strengthened with Cristoval's mad fury and Samantha's deadly feline grace.

Cristoval's moves became more desperately emotional, blindly swinging at her in fury. Samantha danced around him in a flutter of ice-blue silk, swinging both swords at him from different angles, and was rebuffed again. She moved faster but she was beginning to falter, her moves hesitating just a touch. Cristoval sensed it, moving away a step.

"She's losing," Ryan murmured, and glanced across the chamber to the platform where Freitas still hid in the shadows. He could see she had pulled her gun and had it aimed at Cristoval from an elevated position, still half hidden in her cloak.

Danny followed his gaze. "Tell me that is who I think it is," he whispered.

"Won't work, we'll never make it out of here," Ryan replied.

The tip of Cristoval's sword sliced into Samantha's left leg, drawing a thick line of blood. She staggered back, limping as the blood stained the blue silk of her garment.

"Samantha!" Danny cried.

Sensing victory, Cristoval lunged forward.

At the last second, another power surged through Samantha. It was nearly visible, welling up inside her. She dodged Cristoval's sword and drove a scimitar into his chest from the side.

Cristoval stumbled back, dropping his sword. He fell back onto the steps leading to the main dais, bleeding profusely as he sagged to the floor.

Samantha advanced on him slowly, holding her other scimitar just above his heart.

Zorathenne began to clap, stepping down beside him. "I declare Samantha Crews the victor," she said. "An impressive display, my dear. Now you may kill him and take his place as my consort."

Samantha kept her eyes trained on Cristoval's pale face. He moved a bit, but the scimitar piercing through his body caused agony whenever he moved. Then she turned to look up at Zorathenne.

"I will not be your consort," Samantha said.

Zorathenne's pique rose again. She was not used to having her will balked so often, Samantha sensed. The fury was barely contained within her on the best of days and nothing about this had gone well.

"This *thing* has not served me well," Zorathenne said, dismissing Cristoval with a glare. "None who subverts my will can be spared. Kill him and take his place at my side as we reclaim our city."

Samantha faced Zorathenne, her grip on her scimitar tight and strong as Cristoval writhed and bled beneath her. "I did not come here to join you," she said. "I came to avenge the death of my true consort Daniel Robert Carton. As he lives, my reason for being here has ended and I will take my leave of you."

"A human cannot be a true consort," Zorathenne spat. "If you wanted to keep the human as a pet, I would allow it, as long as you belong to me."

Danny whispered to Ryan, "Do I get a say in this?"

"Shush," Ryan returned.

"I belong to no one," Samantha said, her voice rising. She seemed taller somehow, stronger, as she mounted the steps to face Zorathenne. Her scimitar was lowered but that sense of power remained strong, as though there were something more enveloping her. "I do not belong to Cristoval. I shall not belong to you."

Zorathenne glared at her. "I will have one of you, my dear."

"Yes, without a consort, you lose your grip completely, don't you?" Samantha said, that half smile returning. "I will take my people with me and go, and in return I will not deprive you of your consort."

In her mind, Samantha could sense Ryan's fury at her words, barely checked. Samantha glanced down at Cristoval, still pinned by the scimitar, glaring up at her with incendiary hate. "Leaving him under your thumb…that is a far greater punishment than any I could devise," she said. "He may have served you poorly. But I imagine this humiliation will remind him of his place."

Zorathenne shook her head. "He is not as powerful as you, my child. None will leave. I need you by my side."

In a lightning-fast move, Samantha flicked her scimitar up to Zorathenne's neck. The vampires swelled out of the platforms but Samantha merely held the scimitar against Zorathenne's lovely dark neck, barely pressing into the skin.

"I am more powerful than you know," Samantha whispered. "If I remain here, it will not be to join you. It will be to defeat you. And you know I can do it."

Zorathenne met her eyes and for the first time Samantha did not drop her gaze. Will clashed against will and met in the center. The murmuring rose but everyone remained still for a moment.

Then Samantha stepped back, lowering her sword. "We all go," she repeated. "My people. Humans and vampires. We will leave and no one will know you are here. We will declare a truce, you and I, and let no one else pay the price for our petty squabbles."

Zorathenne faced Samantha, her dark gaze boring into Samantha's crystal-blue eyes.

You are a leader, Samantha's mind whispered to Zorathenne. *Choose the best course for your kiss. I will choose for mine.*

"A kiss of humans," Zorathenne said aloud, her voice filled with disdain. "They are pets and playthings. They are food, not consorts."

"Family," Samantha returned. "And they are mine to protect."

Zorathenne slowly nodded. "You may take your humans and the vampire who was vanquished," she said. "But Andrew must remain."

Samantha shook her head. "All my people go with me."

"He belongs to my kiss now, forever," Zorathenne said. "You need not fear for him. He will return to the surface soon enough, live his life as he wishes, much as others under my thrall do. I could not release him now if I wish it, you know that. And his influence will do me no good if he loiters here with my companions."

Samantha glanced over at Drew, who stared at her in silent misery. "I'm sorry," she whispered.

Ryan and Danny came down to the center, joined by Freitas, stepping out of the shadows to no small surprise from the vampires. Samantha stepped down from the dais and knelt beside Cristoval.

"I imagine you think you will get another chance at me or my people," Samantha said softly, too softly for any but Zorathenne to hear. "Instead, I want you to remember this moment."

Cristoval glared up at her in hate. Samantha rested her hand on the scimitar still protruding from his body. Then she twisted it hard, and felt it grind inside him. He threw back his head in agony, but no sound came from his mouth.

"I have beaten you," Samantha said quietly. "If you ever come to the surface again, I will kill you. You know now that I can do it. Look at me." He glared back at her, still silent. "I am your death, Cristoval."

Then Samantha stood and turned to the three standing in the center of the room. In a flash Danny's arms were around Samantha and they held each other in silence. In that moment, Samantha felt something heal in her that had broken, as though reconnecting to a part of herself that had died. She felt his warm hands pressing against her back, his living breath on her shoulder, the shaking of his muscles as he clung to her.

How sweet, Diego whispered to her. *Your boy is safe. I didn't think you could do it, Miranda.*

Samantha's eyes widened. *You? You were with me?*

I am always with you, Miranda, Diego cackled inside her head. *I thought you knew that.*

Ryan crossed the chamber to the dais where Cristoval lay bleeding on the floor. He knelt beside him, fury in every muscle. His hand gripped the handle of the scimitar, still protruding from Cristoval's chest. Blood was pouring freely from Cristoval's chest, the wound that Samantha had made so much worse. A direct stab to the heart would kill him as weakened as he was.

For a moment, Samantha wanted to look the other way. Let him do it. But the rustle of the vampires surrounding them, the thought of what would happen if Cristoval died and Zorathenne's power over them was broken—

"Ryan," Samantha warned, and she put a bit of this newfound power behind it. Just a touch, just to nudge him. "We have an agreement."

Ryan stared into Cristoval's eyes, remorseless and staring beneath him. Ryan's entire body clenched into one taut muscle. His fist tightened on the scimitar handle as he leaned over Cristoval.

Then he reached over and pulled Isabel's claddagh ring none too gently from Cristoval's finger.

"Some day," Ryan said, grim promise in his voice.

Epilogue

The snow was falling again.

It drifted between the bare branches of the trees in Saint Bartholomew's small cemetery, riding the chilled breeze past the wrought iron gates to the small group of people standing in the fading translucent light of a winter afternoon.

Most of the figures dressed in somber overcoats were leaving, shaking Father Stubblefield's hand and talking in muted voice as they trudged back to the lines of cars along the street behind Saint Bartholomew's. A few paralegals from the law firm, a handful of old friends. Duane Russell was there, silent in the back of the crowd, and left without speaking.

Samantha and Danny waited by the gate. Samantha had a thick white bandage around her left leg beneath her black skirt and Danny's head was bandaged. They stood beside Freitas and Parker, who were both in full dress uniform. Parker was still on crutches, a brace supporting her injured leg, but she stood tall beside her partner. Parker was still pale and Flanigan hovered behind her with Fradella and Chapman, all silent and still.

One solitary person remained by the grave, shrouded in his long dark coat.

Ryan Callahan laid a hand on Isabel Nelson's coffin, his face hidden from the small group that waited by the gate. The wind blew his hair back from his face. As Samantha watched, she could see Ryan speaking, muttering something none of them could hear to the silent coffin.

Lining the street beyond the cemetery stood the vampires of Nocturnal Urges and the street kids from the community center. Isabel's coworkers were the first to leave. The rest waited in silent vigil as Ryan stood alone in the snow.

Father Stubblefield started to walk back toward the grave but Samantha laid a hand on the priest's arm and shook her head. Her eyes filled with tears, staring at Ryan, and Danny slid his arm around her shoulder in comforting embrace.

Ryan knelt beside the coffin, his hand still pressed against the shining dark mahogany. His other hand rested over the claddagh ring, which he wore on a chain around his neck. He laid his forehead against the coffin, his mouth still moving in silent words and whispers. Then he stood and turned away to walk back toward the gate.

They waited for him in silence.

As he reached Samantha and Danny, Ryan glanced over and saw Celia, perched up on the hill where the community center had stood with Sensei's small form standing beside her. She was wearing the black dress she had worn to the Christmas party eons ago. Beside her, in front of the charred wreck that had once been the community center, a makeshift sign had been hammered into the ground.

FUTURE SITE OF THE ISABEL NELSON COMMUNITY CENTER

Ryan stopped and stared up at the sign. Samantha squeezed his arm and nodded in response to his questioning gaze.

"It was the least we could do," she said softly.

It was only then that Ryan finally began to cry, his shoulders shaking. Samantha held him with Danny standing close behind her. Freitas and Parker stood by, almost at attention, letting him grieve in the company of family. Ryan's hand stole up to wrap around the claddagh ring, which rested on a chain around his neck.

The snow fell, blanketing them all in its pure white silence.

Author Note

Of course, there was no vampire massacre in Memphis in 1873. But there was a terrible yellow-fever epidemic that caused great panic throughout the city. As far as I know, no particular group was singled out as being responsible for the Memphis epidemic. It would be decades before anyone discovered that yellow fever is spread by mosquitoes, which quite deserve any retribution we can visit upon them.

There is no Saint Bartholomew's Church in Memphis at the time of this writing. I chose the name in commemoration of the Saint Bartholomew's Day Massacre in France in 1572, in which thousands of French Protestants died—another example of hatred and intolerance leading to violence in human history.

There is, however, Saint Mary's Episcopal Cathedral and the Martyrs of Memphis.

During the yellow fever epidemic in 1873, the nuns of Saint Mary's stayed in town rather than evacuate. Without medical training, they nursed the sick and manage to save all but eight of the fifty or so in their care. Following the tradition of Saint Mary's Cathedral since its founding, the nuns cared for the poor and destitute, the forgotten ones whom no one else would notice, the ones who could not flee for higher ground.

Five years later the epidemic returned at ten times its fury. The panic drove out all the wealthy while the poor were left to suffer. The plague so decimated the city that it lost its charter in 1879 and Memphis didn't really recover completely for another twelve years.

Once again the nuns of Saint Mary's stayed to serve their community. Some who were traveling at the time the epidemic struck actually returned to help out. They turned an orphanage for black children into a hospital, providing for all the sick regardless of race or religion. They found homes for the children orphaned by the epidemic and worked as nurses and burial detail.

And they died. Five nuns and a priest. They are known as the Martyrs of Memphis, felled by the very fever they had fought twice. They stayed when others fled. They saved those who society discarded. They carried on the work of healing in the face of their own deaths, some of them quite young.

It is said they still haunt the passages of Saint Mary's Cathedral, which stands today as a beautiful white citadel in what is now downtown Memphis. If they remain, they are friendly ghosts, reminding us of the sacrifice they made and our responsibilities to each other. The people of Saint Mary's carry on their legacy of social service and open arms to this day, holding their own in the face of poverty and violence, welcoming all within their doors and reaching out regardless of race, religion or creed.

It has been my great privilege to know them and their mission.

Also by Elizabeth Donald

ಇಲ

A More Perfect Union

Nocturnal Urges

If you are interested in a spicier read (and are over 18), check out the author's erotic romances at Ellora's Cave Publishing (www.elloracave.com).

Tandem

About the Author

ಇಲ

Elizabeth Donald is a writer fond of things that go chomp in the night. She is the author of the award-winning Nocturnal Urges vampire mystery series and numerous short stories and novellas in the horror, science fiction and erotica genres. By day, she is a newspaper reporter in the St. Louis area, which provides her with an endless source of material. Her web site is www.elizabethdonald.com, and readers can find out more by joining her Yahoo Group at

groups.yahoo.com/group/elizabethdonald.

Elizabeth welcomes comments from readers. You can find her website and email address on her author bio page at www.cerridwenpress.com.

Tell Us What You Think

We appreciate hearing reader opinions about our books. You can email us at Comments@EllorasCave.com.

Why an electronic book?

We live in the Information Age — an exciting time in the history of human civilization, in which technology rules supreme and continues to progress in leaps and bounds every minute of every day. For a multitude of reasons, more and more avid literary fans are opting to purchase e-books instead of paper books. The question from those not yet initiated into the world of electronic reading is simply: *Why?*

1. ***Price.*** An electronic title at Ellora's Cave Publishing and Cerridwen Press runs anywhere from 40% to 75% less than the cover price of the exact same title in paperback format. Why? Basic mathematics and cost. It is less expensive to publish an e-book (no paper and printing, no warehousing and shipping) than it is to publish a paperback, so the savings are passed along to the consumer.

2. ***Space.*** Running out of room in your house for your books? That is one worry you will never have with electronic books. For a low one-time cost, you can purchase a handheld device specifically designed for e-reading. Many e-readers have large, convenient screens for viewing. Better yet, hundreds of titles can be stored within your new library — on a single microchip. There are a variety of e-readers from different manufacturers. You can also read e-books on your PC or laptop computer. (Please note that

Ellora's Cave does not endorse any specific brands. You can check our websites at www.ellorascave.com or www.cerridwenpress.com for information we make available to new consumers.)
3. ***Mobility.*** Because your new e-library consists of only a microchip within a small, easily transportable e-reader, your entire cache of books can be taken with you wherever you go.
4. ***Personal Viewing Preferences.*** Are the words you are currently reading too small? Too large? Too… ANNOYING? Paperback books cannot be modified according to personal preferences, but e-books can.
5. ***Instant Gratification.*** Is it the middle of the night and all the bookstores near you are closed? Are you tired of waiting days, sometimes weeks, for bookstores to ship the novels you bought? Ellora's Cave Publishing sells instantaneous downloads twenty-four hours a day, seven days a week, every day of the year. Our webstore is never closed. Our e-book delivery system is 100% automated, meaning your order is filled as soon as you pay for it.

Those are a few of the top reasons why electronic books are replacing paperbacks for many avid readers.

As always, Ellora's Cave and Cerridwen Press welcome your questions and comments. We invite you to email us at Comments@ellorascave.com or write to us directly at Ellora's Cave Publishing Inc., 1056 Home Avenue, Akron, OH 44310-3502.

Cerridwen Press
Monthly Newsletter

News
Author Appearances
Book Signings
New Releases
Contests
Author Profiles
Feature Articles

Available online at
www.CerridwenPress.com

Cerridwen Press

Cerridwen, the Celtic goddess of wisdom, was the muse who brought inspiration to storytellers and those in the creative arts.

Cerridwen Press encompasses the best and most innovative stories in all genres of today's fiction.

Visit our website and discover the newest titles by talented authors who still get inspired—much like the ancient storytellers did…

once upon a time.

www.cerridwenpress.com